Human Again
Cryonemesis Book 1

A dystopian sci-fi novel

By
Moran Chaim

Find me at
Moranchaim.com

Email me at
moranchaimbooks@gmail.com

Edited by TR Perri
www.trperri.com

Cover design by Eloise J. Knapp
www.ekcoverdesign.com

ISBN 978-965-92549-10

Thank you for purchasing my debut novel!

I would love to know what you think of it.

So, if you like this book please leave a review on Amazon or Goodreads.

Yours,

Moran Chaim.

"Time imprisons us, but civilization enslaves us."

TR Perri

4

Table of contents

Chapter 1

First there was nothing. No sight, no sound, no smell, no taste, no touch. Not even blackness, just infinite emptiness. Then there were sounds of screaming and the smell of burned flesh. Then the taste of blood and a blinding white light. After that came fear, anger and sadness. Then came pain and cold, and there was also a name – Roy.

Was I Roy? As my awareness grew I slowly realized I was attached to a body. A strobing pain of ten thousand organs charging with electricity appeared. I was cold and motionless under the white light.

That was my existence for awhile. I felt my consciousness trying to move but the body didn't respond, like I was swimming in a pool of black oil. My organs were too soft. I floated inside my body, trying to find a firm limb to hold onto as a leaning point. It got warmer pretty fast, but the strobing electricity didn't stop flushing me with pain. It was as if I was being Tasered by a thousand little needles. I don't know how long I was lying in that state. Thin tubes were coming out of me.

"Take cover! Incoming!"

The smell of burned flesh mixed with black smoke and dust. What happened? Was I dead? My jelly body became more firm with each strobe of current. My self-awareness of Roy got sharper as I found my place in the motionless body. My fingertips sensed a wet, plastic surface and my eyes saw figures hovering above me, beneath the blinding brightness. Everything started to make sense. I was Roy. I wasn't dead but I was supposed to be. I tried to take a deep breath but it felt like knives resided in my lungs, so I waited. Parents, I had parents: did they think I was dead? A great sadness overflowed me. Tears ran down the side of my face while I was lying face-up, but I didn't truly understand what I was crying about.

One day I woke up groggy and the incubator tubes were gone. The walls and ceiling were gray, but the light from the ceiling was warm and dimmed, like it came from the sun. I just lay there and looked at the light. I dozed and reawakened a few times before realizing I was in a hospital. A bunch of doctors wearing green and purple overalls were observing me and the monitors I was connected to.

"Where am I?"

"You are safe," said a doctor who approached me. He spoke rather fast.

My mind was slow and my body was aching and shivering.

"I'm cold."

It was weird hearing my voice. It felt distant, like it wasn't mine at all.

"It's normal. Don't worry about it."

"Why are you talking so fast?"

"I'm sorry," he said more slowly, "I forgot you people speak slowly."

I had a bad feeling about this guy but I couldn't do much about it.

"Where am I? Did you tell my parents I am here?"

He looked at his colleagues and then at a mirror that was covering the wall to my left. I started to realize something was off. I raised my head and examined the mirror. He noticed and got closer.

"I need to examine your eye movement and reflexes, please."

I looked at the shape of my body under the blanket to see if I had lost a limb. All seemed intact. A big relief.

"Where am I?"

He raised one finger in the air in front of me and started moving it slowly from left to right in front of my eyes. I followed his finger reluctantly.

"How long was I out?"

"I don't really know."

His answer didn't strike me as odd. I just ignored it.

"Did you tell my parents where I am?"

"Your parents have put you here, so to speak."

"So where are they?"

"Roy, can you please squeeze my hand with your right palm."

I did. I felt weak.

"Just tell me what's going on, I can take it."

Again he looked at his colleagues and at the mirror. He seemed nervous.

"You were cryogenically frozen."

"What do you mean by that?"

"That's all I can say right now. Please squeeze my hand with your left palm."

The whole room was spinning. I gripped the bed frame and looked at the floor so I could focus on something static. I began to hyperventilate.

"You can relax; I am here to help you. We all are," he said gesturing to the other doctors.

A hand with a cup of water entered my field of view. I drank it and then puked on the floor.

"Sorry."

"This is pretty normal. Please try to lie down," the doctor said, putting his hand on my back. Another doctor came by to clean up my vomit splatter.

"Where am I, and where are my parents and friends?"

"You are now in a city called New Knaan. This is a clinic."

"What?"

The room was no longer spinning, so I sat up. My body ached and my head throbbed, making it hard to concentrate on a single thought.

The so-called doctors kept looking at me. I looked at the mirror and saw my face. I was skinny and pale. My eyes were pink with purple undertones and my cheekbones were visible. How long was I out?

And then it hit me.

"Is this Lebanon…are you Hezbollah?"

"Roy, you are safe, please calm d—."

"—ARE YOU HEZBOLLAH?!"

"We are not going to harm you."

"So what is this mirror for? Who's behind it?"

"Just people who are excited to meet you."

"Who? Where are my parents? My friends? Where's Hadar?"

"I'm sorry but they are not here currently, Roy."

"Stop saying my name like you know me. Let me out."

"Please calm down."

"I want out. I need air. Can't you open a window?"

My body felt warmer and more responsive, allowing me to slide off the bed onto the cold, concrete floor. The whole room was made out of ugly gray concrete. No windows. The doctor said I was underground. He was obviously lying. I must have been taken captive by Hezbollah and they were playing a sick trick on me. I didn't see guns so I figured I had just one chance to go out of the door before they chained me to the bed or something. I had to show them I was calm.

"Can I get more water please?"

Again, one of the men handed me a cup of water. He wore a subtle smile, like he was embarrassed of me. I drank and returned the cup to him, and at the moment he moved his hand to take it I grabbed his arm and twisted it behind his back so he couldn't move. I didn't have enough strength to hold him for much longer, but I was able to put enough pressure on his joints to make him motionless and not resistive.

They all looked at me in shock, waving their hands. I then put my other hand on the poor guy's neck.

"Open this door or I'll break his neck."

"The door is open. Please calm down," the doctor said quickly again.

"Stop talking fast! What is this?"

The purple doctor whispered something to the ponytail doctor standing next to him. He stepped back and reached for a tray.

"What is he doing? Tell him to stop."

"Roy, please, let him go. We are not Hezbollah." He was trying to calm me down by speaking slower, but it didn't work.

"How can I trust you? Why am I here?"

I heard running noises from outside, and some commotion. Soldiers might've been coming.

"Like I said…"

I didn't want to listen. I threw my captive at the main doctor and leaped to the door.

"Give him the shot," I heard the purple doctor say. I looked back and saw the ponytail doctor holding a syringe-shaped object.

I opened the door and stepped outside. I didn't see any soldiers yet so I started running down the long corridor. My muscles were rusty and so were my reflexes. The walls were made of the same gray concrete, and the ceiling let in light through a narrow window that stretched above the corridor. People in overalls looked at me as if I were a crazy person, and stepped aside. There were white doors and each door was signed in a language I didn't recognize. My body ached and I could feel my heart pumping hard in my chest. I didn't have the power to run fast enough before they could catch me, but I ran anyway. My muscles betrayed me and I stumbled down and hit a man wearing green overalls. I regained my balance and helped him up.

"I'm sorry," I said, panting heavily.

Once I stood up and started to run again, the floor turned red and I was hit hard in the back, which knocked me to the ground. People all around were staring at me. As I looked back I saw a man dressed in white holding a strange, glowing gun and next to him, the ponytail doctor holding the syringe. I pushed off his arm with my left hand and knocked his chin in with my right hand. He was stunned and rolled to the floor.

I stood up again and kept running in the same direction, though it felt like I was running in a circle because everything looked the same.

"Stop!" shouted the man with the gun.

I had to keep running and oddly he didn't shoot me. I kept running until I reached a giant metal blast door that had another regular door to the side of it. It didn't have any handle on it so I banged as hard as I could.

"Let me out! Please, let me out!"

The floor turned red again, and I immediately turned around and prepare myself for impact. The ponytail doctor was there, holding the syringe device. This time blood was running from his mouth, broken teeth probably. Behind him stood five guards dressed in white overalls holding the same glowing guns. I raised my hands to surrender. My body was shaking from unused adrenaline, and cold sweat ran down my spine.

The ponytail doctor came close to me, and I couldn't resist anymore.

"You must help us."

I felt a strong sting in my neck and that's the last thing I remember.

Chapter 2

I opened my eyes again. This time, I was lying on a patch of soft green grass on top of a hill overlooking the sea. To my right was an old man in khaki shorts and a blue buttoned shirt. He was sitting on a beach chair taking in the view. Everything was dead quiet. I couldn't even hear the sound of the wind.

"Where am I?"

"As Doctor Ashish tried to tell you, the first question should be 'when'."

"Why can't anyone give me a straight answer? And what kind of name is Ashish?"

I stood up and faced the old man. He kept smiling from his chair, not even looking at me, which made me angrier. Finally, he stood up and faced me.

"You can call me Isaac," he said while extending his arm.

"You don't speak fast?"

"Only native Knaan people speak fast. You'll get used to it."

I extended my hand to shake his, but he grabbed my arm next to the elbow and shook that instead.

"This is how we shake now. It's more personal."

I released his grip and put my hands in my pockets. Only then I noticed that I was wearing white overalls that resembled what the guards wore. They looked like a combat pilot's suit.

"Before I start to explain anything, I just have to ask you if you want to be here."

"Here where?"

"Whenever somebody is thawed they have the right to regret it. People like you and me—"

"—What do you mean like 'you and me'?"

"Defrosties, people from the past that were kept in cryogenic freeze."

"What is that?"

"A few hundred years ago, people wanted to reach a point where science and medicine were so advanced that it would heal them from illness and prevent the effects of aging. So they kept themselves frozen until that time came."

"Are you telling me that I'm in the future now?"

"To put it straight, yes."

I felt nauseous. I had to sit down.

"My friends? My parents?"

He crouched down beside me and put his hand on my shoulder.

The tears that rolled down my cheeks earlier started to make sense—I cried over all the people and things I'd lost. My friends, my parents, my little sister, my unit friends that were with me in the last night in Lebanon, Hadar my ex-girlfriend, who probably wasn't contacted by anyone smart enough to let her know I died, my dreams and plans to finish the army and travel the world, to study something, to become somebody important. They used to say that crying releases you from sadness, but I felt like I was drowning in my own swamp of tears. Isaac remained seated next to me that whole time until there were no more tears left. He gave me a tissue to wipe my face.

After a long silence and slow breathing I told him I needed answers. I still didn't know who he was and if he was really telling the truth.

"Where do I go now? What should I do?" I asked.

He looked at me with compassionate eyes, and then something strange happened. I began to feel lighter, as if I was floating through the air. I looked at my feet and they were five inches above the grass. He was floating above his chair, too, sitting in the air and smiling at me like an arrogant Buddha statue.

"There's no need to go anywhere, because your feet don't exist here."

"Is this the afterlife?"

He laughed and grabbed my hand. We launched through the air so fast my guts were pushed to my pelvis. The wind dried my face, and I closed my eyes. I screamed like a baby.

"Isn't it fun?" he said with sadistic intonation.

"No!" I shouted as hard as I could. And then we stopped right in the middle of the sky. We were floating above the whole Middle East like drifting astronauts looking at earth from above. I might have wet my pants. I grabbed his arm tighter. Everything looked like a desert beneath us. Africa. Europe. Israel. Everything was brown and yellow.

"You can let go, you won't fall."

"Are you sure?" I answered, and then let go of his hand.

"Do you recognize this view?"

"It's the Middle East. It's all so dry."

"Besides that, see anything strange about it?"

"Everything looks like a satellite image."

"Don't you think Italy looks too small?"

I looked towards Europe and then I saw it. Italy was narrower, Cyprus was smaller. The whole Israeli coastline was smaller. The sea was bigger. We started descending slowly to the ground, like we were zooming in on a picture.

"I am not going to tell you the whole story, but earth has changed since you left it. Temperatures rose, and so did the sea level. It became impossible to survive on the ground. That's why a group of smart people decided to build New Knaan."

"That's where we are now?"

"When you woke up you were staying in an actual room inside Knaan. But we are now in a simulation that is connected to your brain. We experience it just like real life."

"How long have you been here?" I asked him.

"I was defrosted about ten years ago, born in 2024. So you're older than me technically."

It was the first time I smiled that day. We continued to descend and I started to marvel at the view.

"Why did you preserve yourself?"

"I lost hope in the world back then. I decided to go to sleep until it was over."

"What about your wife and children?"

"That's another story, perhaps for another time."

"But why are we in the simulation now?"

"Usually defrosties are given a tour of the city and introduced to all the different sections and managers. But you made quite a fuss back there so we took a different approach."

We continued our descent and floated towards the hill we were on before. This time, I saw Zeppelins with wind turbines installed on them. I saw solar panels and buildings sticking out of the water over at what used to be Tel Aviv.

"Did all this actually happen in the real world?"

"Oh yes, and much worse. Knaan was built to survive a thousand years, until the earth cooled down again. We make our energy out of wind, sun and sea currents. The energy enables our food production, water desalination, light, air conditioning and simulation."

"So you are not just in my head?"

"I'm real but your experience isn't, so to speak, your brain makes it real."

"Huh…" It made sense, sort of.

"People can't live underground like ants for too long. So they decided to build this simulation where you can do whatever you want."

The whole mountain became transparent and I could see the structure of the city like a 3D model. It was round, like a giant doughnut inside the mountain. The doughnut was as big as a skyscraper lying on its side. There were many pipes and corridors that connected to other smaller rooms on both sides.

"This is where we eat, drink, sleep and work to maintain all the systems that sustain us."

Suddenly, the whole world turned black and I awoke in a small cement room. I was wearing the white overalls, and I was pale and skinny, unlike in the simulation. Isaac was lying on a bed next to me wearing orange overalls. The simulation bed looked like a sleeping pod with a gray plastic lid over it. The headrest was riddled with wires and electrodes. Not as hi-tech as I expected it to be. The lights flickered a few times and then shut down. A small emergency light was turned on.

"I hate when that happens," he said.

"What happened?"

"Oh, the systems aren't very stable these days."

I stood up and surveyed the room. "I thought the future would look different."

"Me, too. The future has no spaceships, no aliens, no flying cars, no teleporting or eternal life or other fancy stuff, just these walls and a simulation to keep you sane."

"How's that working for you?" I asked sarcastically, since I felt like I was reborn in a prison. Sanity was not an option.

"I'm a storyteller, that's my job now. I tell the kids about the past and how to learn from it so they'll know better when they rebuild society on ground."

"Rebuild? When is that coming?"

"No one knows."

It all seemed so strange to me. A rich person could pay to be resurrected in what they believed would be the utopic future, yet accept how shitty it is once they got there. Something didn't make sense.

"That's all you do?" I asked.

"There isn't anything else I can do. You and I, we are too slow for native Knaanians. Their people were born here with quantum computers and simulations since day one. We are too slow to work on those systems."

"So, I am to replace you as a storyteller?"

"Eventually, yes, but no one expected to find someone as young as you. The main reason they keep us is to test the simulation. To make sure it's the same as reality. Because we were born outside it, we can still see the bugs."

"We're lab rats, then?"

"That's actually the fun part."

"That doctor told me that my parents put me here. Why would they do that to me?"

"I don't know, kid, maybe they hoped to give you a second chance."

"Telling stories and being a lab rat doesn't sound like much of a life to me."

He seemed to have taken it personally. But I was too busy processing my own emotions to care about him.

"Listen," he said, "the simulation software is the only technology they can actually develop here. Everything else has been stuck for decades. There is no global trade of electronics and information anymore. They can't build new stuff, only improve the existing."

"And the stories? Why can't they just record some hologram instead of you?"

"That's my benefit. I get to do it myself and they get to collect all different stories from different people. The different angles give them a fuller picture. Plus, it helps them understand what the core of all that went wrong was."

"I was just a teenager, then a soldier. I can't remember much of my life to tell. It's not interesting."

"You died, so you've seen the suffering and war like I did. This is why they defrost us one by one; to teach the children right from wrong."

"And what if I don't want to teach kids?"

He turned to another bed where another person lay under the hood.

"Then you could be like this guy here, who chose to assimilate into the simulation and never wake up."

"He's locked inside his own head?"

"Inside his infinite fantasy. Not a bad state to be in, but I'd choose the real world over assimilation anytime."

"What happened to him during the power outage?"

"A little sedation comes into play to keep him under until the problem is fixed."

I stepped to examine the assimilated guy's bed. I couldn't see his face but his body posture seemed relaxed. His body twitched from time to time as if he was dreaming. His vitals were displayed in the green spectrum on the little screen attached to the bed.

"What if I don't want to be a storyteller and don't want to assimilate?"

"Then we have a problem because I don't have any answers for you. I guess they'll have to test your skills like the rest of the kids."

"Will you help me?"

He paused.

"Let's eat first."

Chapter 3

I wasn't hungry until Isaac mentioned eating. I realized I hadn't eaten for years. My stomach made those digestion sounds that triggered salivation, and Isaac no doubt heard them. Still sitting on the simulation bed, I wondered what food they produced underground.

"We need to go back inside the simulation," said Isaac.

"The food isn't real?"

"Oh it's real, better than real."

We both slid inside the headrest and closed the lid. It felt weird at first, but in a second we were sitting by ourselves in a fancy restaurant. Chandeliers hung from the ceiling, candles on the tables, a vine fence decorated the outskirts of the sitting area, and we wore 21st-century clothes.

"I hope you like my decorating; I try to have fun with it sometimes."

"You conceived this place?"

"Yes, this is Knaan survival lesson number one. Anything you can think of can be created by your mind inside the simulation, from a famous piece of art to your most dirty fantasy. You can choose to share it with others or not. You create your own world."

"So I can create any food that I want?"

"Exactly, although you don't have to think too hard. Make a mental image or think of the name of the dish you want. Your brain will tell the simulation the rest of it.

"I don't know what I want to eat."

"I've been told that most people choose steak, or spaghetti Bolognese."

"I'll take the spaghetti, then."

In a split second a plate with steamy spaghetti appeared in front of me. It was hot and red, and smelled like meat with fresh tomatoes and basil. Isaac looked at me with intent.

"Eat, don't wait for me."

I took a fork and started swirling the pasta on it. It even sounded like real pasta being swirled around a plate. Some sauce sprayed on my shirt. In the meanwhile, Isaac had produced a bowl of noodle soup that he started to eat with chopsticks and a spoon.

"What's that?" I asked.

"It's called pho, a Vietnamese soup," he said. "Do you want to taste?"

"Can't you like, transmit your thoughts to me?"

"This is lesson number two. I can't transmit my thoughts to other people, or my body to other people's worlds without being invited, or granted permission."

"I allow you to transfer the soup's taste."

My head was filled with different flavors entirely: soy, red chili and a hint of anise. It was if I was eating two dishes simultaneously.

"What about learning? Can you transfer knowledge directly to my brain?"

"Learning is a deep and complex process. For you to own a memory or ability it has to be shown or taught. Your brain needs to create physical neural connections in order to create learning."

I took another bite. The pasta was delicious. The sauce filled my body with warmth and energy. I felt like I was regaining my strength, and was becoming more relaxed. But then it hit me.

"Wait..." I stopped eating.

Isaac smiled like he knew what I was about to say.

"What am I really eating? This isn't pasta, right?"

He smiled.

"Is it?" I asked again.

"The simulation tells your brain it is."

"So what do I eat in reality?"

He hesitated.

"The bed is equipped with a little straw that slides the food down into your mouth."

"What food?"

He hesitated again.

"Do you want to know? Or do you prefer just eating normally?" he asked, gesturing to our feast.

"I want to know everything about this place."

He held a piece of green onion with his chopsticks and ate it.

"Well, you asked for it. You sure you don't want to grab another bite before I tell you? You might lose your appetite."

I dropped my fork to the table and looked at him with a straight face.

"Just tell me."

"It's a mixture of algae, jellyfish and bugs."

I coughed out the chunk I was chewing.

"What bugs?" I asked with disgust.

"What does it matter? It's the best source of protein you can find underground, and the only thing we can farm."

"That's disgusting!"

"You get used to it. Focus on your pasta." He slurped more noodles from his bowl.

"I think I'll pass on that. So how is water made?"

"Water is water, we desalinate it from the sea."

"Are you sure it's not recycled piss or bug juice?"

Isaac laughed.

"I'm sure. Trust me; we don't get a lot of showers down here. Water is not something we make jokes about."

"So how do you clean yourself?"

"Germs, there are special germs that live on your body and keep you clean and not smelly."

"I'm starting to see why people choose to assimilate."

"Well, you wanted to hear the truth."

"What about bathrooms? What if I pee on this table right now?"

"Then you'd be peeing in your bed and stinking up the room we are in."

"With all this technology couldn't they figure out a way to feed us and to have a bathroom in the same place?"

"They could, but would you sit naked inside it and let a machine wipe your ass for you?"

"But you said people who assimilate never get out."

"If you hook on intravenous feeding and a urine collector you can stay inside."

"Ok, you win." I finally gave up, lifted my fork and took another bite.

"The third lesson of Knaan survival is how to use the toilets. But first, there is another reason why learning how to create food is important."

"Let's hope it's not as disgusting."

"You lost your family and friends. Although they lost you a long time ago, for you they still exist. The simulation works on people just like it works on food."

"I can re-create my family?"

"Yes, the simulation will create them from your memories and you'll be able to talk to them and get closure."

"But it won't be real."

"It'll be real for your mind. I will wait for you outside. Come out when you're ready. And I'll show you how to flush a toilet."

"Wait!" I called, but Isaac was already gone. I didn't know what to do alone in the simulation. Am I to talk with my dead friends now, with my parents? Tell them I am sorry I died? That I missed them? That I wish they didn't suffer? I felt weird. For me it was just a day gone. For them it might have been weeks of sadness. I was sent to protect my country, but I failed. I didn't return home safe. The country was saved anyway. Isaac didn't tell me otherwise. I didn't know how to feel. I had too much information to process and I couldn't believe anything he told me. Maybe I wasn't dead, and this wasn't the future at all. Nothing made sense. It all felt like a dream. Maybe I was still going through surgery and this was my hallucination under the anesthesia.

I just couldn't do it. It was too much to take on. So I quit the simulation.

Isaac seemed surprised that I didn't stay.

"I can't," I said.

"That's ok, whenever you're ready. You know what to do," he said before sitting down on his bed.

I took a long, long breath. I had to focus. It all felt too overwhelming.

"So what year is it?" I asked.

"2321," he said with pride.

"Wow…" My mind went blank. I couldn't even imagine this gap in time.

"When I was a child," he said, "I expected the world to have hovering skateboards, holograms and laser swords. It didn't happen. So at least I can make it happen in the simulation. You can go crazy without seeing the sun in years…living in a gray room like this one."

"You haven't been outside since you got here?"

"No."

"I'm sorry."

"No one goes outside except security guards. It's too damn hot."

I looked around the gray room, and then at the light that came from the ceiling.

"This isn't natural light, right?"

"Right, it's just mimicking the color."

"I need to know what happened to my family."

"You mean, three hundred years ago?"

"If they put me here they must have been planning to meet me here."

"I never heard about your parents, or about anyone looking for their kid."

"Maybe they're still inside."

"Cryogenics were expensive. Maybe they could only afford it for you."

"It doesn't make sense to me."

He stood up and stretched. "I would love to talk more but I have to go and teach."

"Can I come with you? I don't really have anything else to do."

"To be honest, I think you might scare the kids," he said, smiling. "Maybe after the color returns to your cheeks, yeah?"

And the old bastard left me in that gray room.

Chapter 4

I did cry again after he left; you can't help but feeling alone and isolated from everything. At the time I couldn't grasp the meaning of waking up three hundred years in the future. Maybe it was a defense mechanism that prevented me from realizing my terrible situation in its full scale. I felt like I had enough simulation time for one day and I didn't want to drift away to old memories again so I stepped outside.

I started walking around, staring at people and things. They stared back. I didn't know what to say and if I should even say anything. I thought, *"Hi, I'm Roy, the new defrosty."* It sounded crazy to say it, even in my own mind. After a few minutes of walking along the curve of the main street, my lungs filled with a mixed smell of rust, mold and stale air. I went looking for the clinic I was in on the first day to find some answers. Eventually I found it after circling the whole city twice. I went inside and saw a bunch of doctors behind the one-way mirror I was being watched by yesterday. They were in the middle of an operation, though instead of using their own arms, they used a robotic arm to dig inside someone's body. A doctor came out to greet me.

"Can I speak with Doctor Ashish?" I asked.

"I'll let him know you're here."

He went back into the surgery room and pressed something that looked like an intercom. I watched the doctors observe the robot hand dissecting the body. Bodies are still bodies, doctors are still doctors. After a moment Dr. Ashish came out from another room. He smiled at me.

"I bet you came to see the cryo lab."

"Yes."

"Come, I'll show you everything."

I followed him into a smaller room with computer screens. They looked like curved, semi-transparent surfaces simply hanging from the ceiling. The keyboard and touch panel were part of the screen and you used it standing up. We passed that control room and got into the cryo lab. There were dozens of metal containers connected to a central hub via wires and pipes. The air was super-cold.

"This is where you came from," he said with pride like he was showing me the facts of life themselves.

"Why did you unfreeze me?"

"You were next in line."

"Yeah, but why?"

"You were next in line, next in queue."

"That's it?"

"Yes, what did you expect?"

"No one asked you to unfreeze me?"

"You were next. We didn't know who you were until we started the process and discovered you were a young man. It was quite a surprise."

"Is there any chance my parents are here?"

"Let's take a look."

We came back to the control room, and he ran a search query.

"Yes, I see there's a notification here about missing parent containers."

"Oh! So they were frozen with me!"

"But they are not here."

He ran the search again. I could realize by the sound of the screen that he found nothing.

"It doesn't make sense," I said. "Why would my parents put me here but not come themselves?"

"Cryogenics was unstable back then. Maybe something went wrong."

"I can't believe they just put me here."

"Maybe something happened and they weren't able to immediately freeze themselves. The global crisis was pretty nasty."

I probably looked helpless, like a boy lost in a public space.

"It doesn't make sense."

"I can try to ask the other cities' doctors. Maybe your parents got there somehow."

"There're more cities like this?"

"Yes, one in the north and one in the south."

He opened a communication window and there was an indication that there was a failure establishing connection.

"I can't access it now. There's probably a sandstorm above us right now, disrupting the signal."

"Are you sure? Can you try again?"

"Trust me; I'll make sure you'll get answers the minute I get them myself."

"Thank you."

I shook his arm and left. I felt hope that I might have someone to belong to after all. I left the clinic and saw a line of guards walking in my direction. As a habit I learned on my first day I stood with my back against the wall to let them pass, although there was plenty of room. I didn't want to get a syringe in my neck again. But, on the other hand, Isaac mentioned that the only ones who go outside were the security guards. That kind of trouble was worth the risk. I had to do something to join them and see what the world had become for real.

The guards passed before me.

"Is everything ok?" I asked the last one of the line.

"*Just routine maintenance.*"

"What maintenance?"

"*Sorry,*" he said, walking faster to avoid me.

"Outside?"

"*Excuse me, kid, I have to…*" and he ran off with the rest of them.

Kid? I could be his great-great-granddad. I kept following the guards until they took a turn into the inner circle of the city. They went up the dark staircase into another room. Their guns' rattle echoed in the narrow corridors. Then they started dressing up in these weird camouflage suits made from thin, metal fibers. First they put on the pants, than the vests, then the sleeves and then the headpieces. They got dressed up pretty fast, and then stepped on a platform that lifted up into the surface. The hatch dilated like a camera's shutter. The light from above was so bright that my eyes shut automatically until they readjusted to the light. When the platform elevator pushed them up it looked like an alien spaceship was abducting them. The metal grinding sound was unpleasant and when it was over I felt a relief. I searched around and quickly found another suit that was left hanging. Was it damaged? Did they not have enough guards to do maintenance? I had to try it on because it was my opportunity to see the outside world, so I dressed up the way they did. The thin metal fibers were so spiky that I had to stop and readjust it every few seconds. It felt like little thorns pierced my skin. How did they do it so quickly? When I finished dressing up, I realized walking in that thing wasn't pleasant either. I made sure no one was coming near the room and went next to the platform, yet nothing moved. A voice from an intercom on the wall barked at me.

"Where have you been? Everyone's already out," she said with judgmental tone.

"Bathroom stop," I said quickly.

"Where's your gun?"

Shit, my gun. What was I thinking? That they will just let me out?

"Someone else took it for me."

"Scan your eyes please."

A red light under the intercom speaker flashed and I hesitated.

"You know what? I think I still don't feel well. Stomach issues."

I turned away and started to remove the suit's parts. By the time I finished and was ready to leave, two other guards were already there to intercept me. They weren't holding any guns, just unfriendly bats.

"Hi, guys," I said while raising my hands in the air like I was about to be arrested, wondering whether I could take them in a fight. Probably not, I hadn't fully recovered yet, but in a few weeks: no problem. One of them took out a pair of handcuffs.

"You must come with us."

"Ok," I said and extended my wrists. I shouldn't cause more trouble on my first day. Or was it the second day? It's not like I actually did something wrong, I was just touring the city and stumbled upon this room.

Before one of the guards cuffed me there was another brief power outage, but before I could escape in the dark, a red light started flashing above our heads. A quiet siren sounded as the platform was lowered, letting the light inside. One guard was holding two wounded guards who were moaning in pain. Blood was dripping off the platform. I could hear gunshots echoing from the outside. The two guards that came for me rushed to take a stretcher off the wall. It wasn't the first time I saw gun wounds.

"What happened?"

"Stand aside, kid!" the stretcher holders shouted.

"Fucking Purists!" said one of the wounded guards. The other one was already unconscious, and they rushed him out of the room.

The wounded guard looked at me like I was an alien and I immediately jumped in and pulled him off the platform. The platform shot up and the room became dark again. I pulled apart the suit around his wound, cutting my hands and mixing my blood with his. He was holding his pain, releasing a little bit of it with every breath. He was in great danger if the bullet hit a main artery. I tried to tear some fabric off my overalls but I was too weak so I just put pressure on his wound with my both arms.

"Don't leave me!" he commanded. Lucky for him, I knew the procedures. A gunshot in the future was still a gunshot. And a gunshot to the thigh can be lethal. I had a chance to do something good, and I liked it.

"Don't worry, you'll be fine," I told him, but I could see he was lost in the pain. I believed my own words, though; if they could resurrect people they could treat gun wounds.

A few seconds later the doctors came and took him away on a stretcher. I noticed their whole crew was looking at me with surprise, so I looked back with fiery eyes: *Yup, it's me again. Same guy who kicked your ass and escaped yesterday. And I'm here to stay.*

I was detained in that room for another half an hour before the guards started coming back from above, all dirty from desert dust and sweat. A cleaning crew dressed in green overalls also came by to wash the muddy blood off. It was then that they finally sent someone to talk to me. She was a slim, elegant woman, wearing white overalls with silver threads woven into them. Her hair was short and neat and her features were strong but welcoming.

"You must be Roy," she said, extending her arm for a shake, which I apprehensively returned.

"I'm President Padma, and I wanted to meet you in person but I didn't think it would be this way."

She didn't sound welcoming at all.

"I wanted to thank you for saving a man's life but you did try to dress up as a guard and go out."

"I did what I had to do."

She didn't seem to care.

"I consider you a child of mine. I try to keep all my children safe. I get disappointed when they disobey the rules, and I get angry when someone puts others at risk."

"I couldn't stay inside, I had to see—"

"—I realize adapting to this place will be hard for you, but you could've gotten yourself killed or kidnapped."

"By whom?"

She paused and studied my face. I studied hers and could feel my old skills come back, though sluggishly.

"I must continue the investigation of this."

I didn't know what to say. I wanted to ask her permission to go out anyway, and I also wanted to know things about this place and about whoever shot the guards. Yet timing matters.

"I won't fail you again."

She smiled like she didn't buy my honesty.

"You need to realize something. You have your old habits and traits still alive in you. But it doesn't work like that here. If you do anything that might put my children at risk one more time I'll have you assimilated."

If that wasn't a threat I don't know what is.

"Get your skills tested tomorrow; we'll find you something productive to do. Or at least acceptable," she added, and then left the room before I could reply.

When Isaac came back to our room that night, I was afraid he'd start lecturing and preaching, but he said nothing, like he didn't even care. Maybe nothing could surprise this old man. Or maybe he was just disappointed in me.

"Tell me about the Purists," I said, trying to break the silence.

"I'm tired. Do you still have your balls attached?" he asked.

So he knew about what happened.

"Tell me about the Purists. I was right there when they shot those guards."

"It's too long."

"You told me you're a storyteller but you sure didn't tell me the whole story about this place. Tell me the truth: the power outage didn't happen out of nowhere, did it?"

This statement got on Isaac's nerves. He sat down on his bed and stroked his knees like he was trying to avoid something that's uncomfortable.

"What do you want to know?" he asked.

"Everything."

"The Purists began in my time. The world's temperatures rose and hunger started to spread because it was harder and harder to farm crops. Climate change was the faceless enemy that turned everyone against each other. Bigger groups looted from smaller groups. So what the Purists first did was teach people how to farm in those extreme conditions. And people started to get dependent on them."

Isaac paused, clearly appraising his fatigue and frustration. But I could tell he really wanted to convey this.

"The Purists gave people seeds and also arranged the bartering between families and groups. They controlled the marketplace and the knowledge in a world of growing chaos and looting. People knew that the Purists would take care of them and keep them safe while all they needed to do was let them handle the exchange between different farms while taking a commission. It all worked well for awhile because they were too small for anyone to supervise, and especially because the world governments and police were crumbling. There was too much going on. No one cared about a bunch of farmers talking about how technology corrupted mankind and how any development is a sin against humanity."

I started feeling heavier in my bed. I was involved in something even bigger than I thought.

Isaac sighed. I could tell he knew he had to tell it all as it was, no more half-truths.

"The world split into two: the few who had and the many who hadn't. The poor were the ones who fought each other like savanna animals. When it became impossible for the Purists to farm, they had to find another way to provide for the people who were depending on them. So they used the sin card and started to raid technological institutes in the name of Purity. When they could steal green technology they claimed it was only for survival means, and that once the atmosphere changed again they'd dispose of it. Every other technology was destroyed and with it the people responsible. Their food was of course looted."

"So they started killing scientists?" I asked.

"Scientists, technicians and associated investors and businessmen."

"And no one stopped them?"

"Who? By the time they started to cause trouble there was no real governing force to deal with them."

"And you still wanted to go under the freeze knowing that they'd try to destroy this place?"

"It was the only safe place to be. They hadn't even finished building it, but I knew there was no other place."

He paused for a moment.

"It's not that I was defrosted here by accident. I care about this place. It saved my wife and me. I won't just assimilate without knowing that I can trust who I leave behind."

He went inside his bed and closed the lid. I felt my eyes go heavier and heavier. The burden of knowing too much wasn't as heavy as my tired body.

I entered the simulation and had to relax. I
wanted a beer. I immediately had a perfect pint of
amber beer in my hand, which I didn't even have to
specify. Cold and refreshing. I thought about the
simulation shooting bug juice or recycled pee in my
mouth. I resisted the urge to vomit and got used to
blocking the idea. After I chugged the beer, I
wondered where to put the glass, but it just
disappeared. Then I wanted to get some air. I looked
at my feet and saw them rise above the ground inch
by inch. I was hovering slowly, just like I did with
Isaac. Now I was the one controlling it. I looked to
my left and hovered left. I looked to my right and
hovered even faster. I looked up and launched
myself 10 feet in the air. It was so cool. I could
actually feel the wind in my face. Then I took off
again. I flew up as fast as I could through the
clouds, diving into and circling them, creating new
shapes with every pass. I wanted to scream out of
joy. What if somebody was listening or monitoring
my brain? I screamed anyway. I felt such a relief. I
didn't care if I died or not. I could fly. I could shoot
a rainbow out of my belly and ride on a flying
unicorn if I wanted. Shit. It actually happened. I

forgot that it wasn't just a metaphor in my head. I found myself riding unicorn with a rainbow coming out of me. I stopped that idea immediately because I didn't want someone to see it.

I wanted to go on the ground somewhere. It's easier to control the situation with a sense of gravity. I looked down and saw how the sea was far away. So I thought *What if I imagine myself there without flying?* After a beat, I was there. It was like turning your head sideways really fast. Your eyes follow slightly slower and suddenly you find yourself standing on a beach. The weather changed a bit; it felt warmer. The waves crashed on the shore. Seagulls flew over my head. I could see some people from afar but they felt like part of the setting. So I sat down on the beach and imagined myself in a bathing suit. There I was, watching the waves on my own private beach. It was so peaceful, but I had one thing missing so I changed the color of the sun to be redder, like the sunset. I took a deep breath. Waves are the kind of things you could look at for hours. Just hearing the soothing sounds of them recede after they lost their energy is meditative.

Fire-gazing is the same. I used to love having campfires outside with my friends. What happened to my friends? I started to remember my last day before dying. I was on a beach like this one, with my two friends. We were sitting on a blanket drinking cheap beer and venting about the army until the beach tennis ball hit me. Beach tennis is a common Israeli activity and a very boring one if you ask me. Instead of trying to score point against each other, you're supposed to bounce the ball to each other and keep it from dropping. Pointless. I turned in its direction and saw a beautiful blonde girl running towards me with a smile.

"Sorry, did I hit you hard?" She was tanned and sweating. She had colorful Indian beads tied to her hair.

"No, I'm ok."

I threw the ball to her and she bounced it with the racket and turned away.

"Idiot, you should've asked for her number in return for the ball."

I turned toward my friend Noam, who was looking at me disappointed.

"She should have given you her number in return for YOUR balls," said Dan.

Noam and Dan were my best high school friends. I knew them for four years, after I had moved to the new school. Now we barely saw one another because we each had different weekends off from the army. Sometimes you stayed for two or three weeks straight and your parents came to visit. Sometimes they were not allowed. Sometimes you were there a whole month until another unit came to replace you.

"Screw it," I said. "I don't have time for a girlfriend anyway."

Was it me saying that? Was that what I said on that actual day? I couldn't remember but I let the simulation lead me. It must have dug into my memories and was showing me how I remembered it.

"You're such a pussy, always with those excuses," said Dan.

"Dude, did you even get laid since you broke up with Hadar?" added Noam.

Hadar, she was my ex. I didn't want to think about her at that moment, there was too much anger and regret involved in that process. I just wanted to relax on the beach.

There was a moment of silence. We all sipped on the beer and looked at the waves. We also looked at the blonde girl. Then Noam said something. I can't tell if he *really* did or if he was just saying that in my head, but it felt like a memory.

"If I die I just want you to know you were my best friends."

"Shut up, you're not going to die," I interrupted.

"Let me finish," he stressed. "If I die, I want happy music at my funeral. Like reggae or something. I don't care if it's against the army rules. You're going to play reggae and people are going to dance."

Dan and I looked at each other.

"I'm serious; you have to promise me that. And if a news crew comes to interview my parents after the funeral, I want you to play reggae there, too. I don't want those terrorists seeing my mom crying on TV."

"If you die, people are allowed to be sad," said Dan.

"Not at my funeral, I'm sick of sad funerals of dead soldiers. Everybody is crying like it was a big surprise that soldiers die in this country. They prepare us from kindergarten to acknowledge that death is possible. So I don't want hypocrisy at my funeral. It was my life and it ended so I want you to celebrate my life. I don't want the terrorists to see you cry and feel that they have won."

I might have said something back to him on that day but suddenly it felt like he had a good point.

"And one more thing," he added.

"What else, you freak?" said Dan.

"I want you to fly to Amsterdam together and smoke a giant ass joint in my memory."

"Let's just say that we'll be here after we're finished with the army, ok?" I said. But I felt like I couldn't talk anymore. My eyes started to get wet and I didn't want them to see it. So I stood up and let the wind dry my eyes. I will never fly to Amsterdam with them. Not in reality at least.

"Sit down, you're blocking the sun," said Noam.

"I'm going to pee," I said.

"Go pee in the water."

"I don't feel like it, do you want another beer?"

"Sure," they both said.

I took my wallet and headed to the bathroom. It smelled as if it hadn't been cleaned for days. I should have peed in the water. It's filled with other people's pee anyway. It's like a common fact that you're allowed to pee in the sea because the salt disinfects your pee, or maybe because pee is salty anyway.

Then I realized I can't pee in the simulation and that I'll have to change my memory and go straight for the beer. I remember being pretty drunk that day and it felt similar in the simulation, that tipsiness. I bought three more beers. Even in the simulation's beach kiosk they ripped me off. When I got back Noam and Dan looked worried. I could see them arguing and packing our stuff.

"What happened? I asked.

"They just kidnapped two more soldiers in Lebanon," Dan said.

"First Gilad Shalit and now these two: we're going to war."

"Stop playing with me," I replied. Little did I know, back then.

"Dude, you had like three calls since you left."

I took out my phone. I had three missed calls and a text message. Before I could open it, the phone rang again. It was my commander.

In the simulation, I jumped forward in time to when I drove to the Wiseman Institute where my father used to work. He was a scientist researching genome stuff that I didn't understand. So If I had anything to do with cryogenic freezing it must have been his idea. I called my mom, who was an officer in the nearby Air Force base.

"Hi, Mom, what's up?" I put her on speaker and tried to be as calm as I could, knowing it's not a good time to stress her with thoughts about war.

"Hi, where are you? They're calling everyone in, did they call you?"

"Yeah, I'm on my way to Dad: he'll take me to Tel Aviv."

"Listen, I hear that this time it's going to be big. I can't talk on the phone but there's more action than usual."

"I know, we can't sit quiet after two kidnappings in two weeks."

"Right, don't be a hero, ok? Be safe."

"I will," I said, realizing that that was the exact opposite of what I was expected to do. My unit mates *were* the heroes; we *were* the stuff you see in movies. Go in, do the job, get out: clean and silent. Nobody knew we were there. Invisible.

"I got to go, hon, talk to me when you can."

She hung up. I didn't tell her I loved her, nor even thanked her, and didn't even say goodbye. She was called on a job, and I also had a job to do. I didn't think about death in those moments. I was filled with a mixture of adrenaline and fear. This was the real deal, the stuff I was training for, for almost two years. I hate to say that but I was somehow excited that shit was going down and I would get some real serious action. I believed it was going to be the same as all the small operations and surveillance hideouts that we used to do. Maybe even slightly bigger and more important. We might even find our soldiers alive, although we rarely do.

I was wrong of course. I went home, showered in like two minutes, put on my uniform

and picked up my M-16 and my army duffle bag
and drove to pick up my dad. He waited for me
outside the main gate. I let him drive because I was
too nervous to drive any more than I had to. He was
wearing his overused checkered blue shirt and had
his reading glasses in the front pocket of the shirt.
He wore green Crocs sandals. He usually didn't talk
much but I could see he was uneasy. We started
driving to Tel Aviv where I was supposed to get on
a bus that would take me to the base next to the
Lebanon border.

"Did you call Mom? She's worried."

"Yeah I did, but she had to go. Everyone is
preparing."

"This time it's the real deal."

"I know." We were so used to having small
incidents we didn't think of them as real.

We kept in silence for a few minutes until we
got on the highway. I didn't know what to say that
wouldn't sound too dramatic or too scared. He
turned on the radio. The news said that the Air
Force had started to attack in Lebanon, and that
Hezbollah was firing rockets at northern cities.

Then he turned the volume down and started talking after a long sigh.

"When will people stop fighting over imaginary inventions like borders and nations, and start fighting for the actual development of the world?" he asked.

My dad was a soldier like the rest of the Israeli men and women, and wasn't a pacifist. He even fought in the first Lebanon war of 1982. But ever since he got into studying genes he had changed. He always reminded us about how tiny and insignificant our daily lives were in comparison to the potential of our evolution, and how we should appreciate our lives more.

"Maybe one day you can remove the fighting gene from people," I said.

"The potential to fight is in our genes but the implication is strictly in the mind. And that is the hardest part to change."

"I am sure you will find the way if you look for it."

"That's not what our funds are for but that's actually an interesting idea."

"Right, I forgot that prolonging the life of rich people is more important because they can pay for it."

He laughed.

"It's not only for rich people; in the short-term maybe, but not in the long-term. Like any invention, it was expensive in the first days, before it became a mass product. Only kings had toilets once. You're a king now.

I laughed; it was a tiny release from the stress that started to build inside me the closer we got to Tel Aviv.

If I only knew how right he was, now that I was revived.

We got to the pick-up point. I could see my Army mates arriving with their parents. It looked like a ritual. Boys are going to war, parents are going back home to be worried and get stuck with news reports. I don't know what's worse: watching the news every day repeating the same stressful items, or being in a void until a phone rings.

He tapped me on the shoulder and said, "Keep safe, don't be a hero."

I walked toward the bus thinking how weird that was. Let's say if I were in WWII. I would want to be a hero and fight the Nazis. I would have gotten a gold medal for that. But here in Israel, we had a nice little war every two or three years. Suddenly being a hero didn't mean anything because no side lost and the wars didn't end. Heroes can't solve all our problems. It's better to survive and go on with your life. So you could say you did your part and let the soldiers of two years from now deal with that shit again. Hoping they won't call you to army reserves, but they usually do.

I sat next to one of my unit friends. We didn't talk for the whole two and a half-hour drive. We stopped to pick up more soldiers on the way north. Nobody talked. Everyone was stressed. Listening to the news didn't help us either. But it's an addiction; you just had to know what's going on. And when they didn't have anything new to say they interviewed another ex-general/politician who was willing to talk about stuff he used to know but now was irrelevant, just to keep the broadcast alive.

I arrived at the base and met with all my unit mates. Everybody started to get pumped up in a

positive way, I would say. The stress that had built
in us had to be released and tunneled into action,
and we were highly trained for that action. The
Hezbollah was a guerrilla organization, also highly
trained. They had hideouts and secret tunnels all
over the mountains and between the villages. They
had cost us many lives each week before Israel
withdrew from Lebanon. Hezbollah soldiers weren't
the ones to throw stones and Molotov cocktails at
you. They were our Viet Cong.

We had a quick debrief with the commanding
officer, and then we went to get equipment. My
commander approached me.

"You could have been an officer-in-training
now."

"I didn't want to become a stinky asshole like
you," I said with a smile.

He gave me a strong pat on the back, the kind
that hurts. It's called a Chapha; it's what men do to
each other in order to show affection by touching in
a manly way.

We sat down for a quick dinner fully
equipped: a protective vest, helmet, ammunition, a
few grenades, and a radio I was supposed to carry

on my back. Some extra batteries also. I remember thinking about who would tell Hadar about me if something happened. I imagined us reuniting after an injury. Or that she was the only one I would allow to see me if I was too fully bandaged. It had been a year since I broke up with her, and I wasn't sure if anyone thought I'd cared to let her know if something happened to me. I wished someone would be smart enough to connect the dots. This caused me to burst out into hot, wet, uncontrollable sobs in the simulation. At that moment, everything in the simulation stopped around me like the memory frozen in time because I couldn't take it anymore. I was back in the simulation bed. I just couldn't re-experience the battle that led to my death. I lost all those people: Noam, Dan, my mom and dad, my sister, who I didn't even have a chance to talk to, my army friends, my commander and my ex. I missed Hadar so much. I wondered if she was sad at my funeral, if she even came and whether it stopped her from dating for a while. And if she thought about me at her wedding or wondered what it would've been like to have kids with me. I wondered if Noam and Dan had kids and what they grew up to be. I wondered if my sister helped my parents in the last days. I wondered if my parents' marriage survived my death or got a divorce out of sadness and growing apart. I wondered how my dad managed to freeze my body and fund it all these years. And why didn't they freeze themselves to meet me here?

I felt so alone the tears didn't stop. My nose ran, and my eyes hurt from squinting so hard. I lost all control of my life and of everything I had. I was in a new world with new rules and new people who had weird names and lived underground, only to survive the climate and be threatened by a crazy radical group. It was the shittiest future anyone could ever predict and I was there to live it.

All these questions gave me a little sense of reality. The tears stopped when the logic kicked in, demanding answers. I lifted the bed's plastic cover. My eyes were wet. My face was wet. Isaac had sat looking at me the whole time. He leaned over and put his comforting hand on my shoulder.

Chapter 5

It was my second day in Knaan. I woke up
and had breakfast in bed, which meant going back
to the simulation and eating breakfast there. I chose
a typical Knaan breakfast, which was manifested
virtually into a chopped salad with lemon, olive oil
and tahini, an omelet with mushrooms and green
onions, and fresh bread with cheese. Isaac ate the
same and was happy with my imaginative cooking
skills. It didn't taste like bugs at all. I didn't want to
think how my breath would smell in reality after
eating that. But he was right: when you're hungry
you don't care about that.

The automated shower was next to the toilet
in the room that held eight simulation beds. It was
automated so people won't waste water. And water
was precious to produce because it needed to be
desalinated. The shower resembled a car wash: you
get in, press start, and water shoots at you from all
directions in thin, strong streams. It's a short burst,
maybe ten seconds. Then you're supposed to lift
your arms so it'll hit your armpits, and spread your
legs to wash your groin. Then you're supposed to

close your eyes and mouth, which you better do because the shower sprays soap all over you. If you don't, it becomes a shower of screams. They were possessive of their soap because of its limited quantity, too. After you're sprayed with soap you have thirty seconds to scrub yourself. You then get ten more seconds of water and then you can dry yourself as much as you want. Due to the fact that showering is such an ordeal, and how the air is filled with germs that are supposed to make you odorless and clean for a few days, most people just don't shower.

Isaac and I were headed to the simulation lab. It's the room where they actually program and monitor the simulations. We took a short cut, and instead of circling the city we cut through a corridor that took us to the opposite side. Less people travelled across there so as to avoid the sound of the pipes pumping water or ventilating air. It was like going into the body of the city and seeing all the veins and arteries, with the wires being the nerve endings. All the simulations were controlled by quantum computers, which were so fast and smart that they could do a gazillion calculations a second.

As such, they could come up with infinite possibilities and results for each problem. I was there because a quantum computer was going to test me for my role in the city. I didn't want to say it out loud, but I thought telling stories was boring. I wanted to do something with my life that affected people. Before I had died, I wanted to learn about mass media, or psychology, or marketing; anything that had a direct effect on people. I wanted to know how to read them better, to know what motivated them and how to drive them to action in a positive way so they could be happier and calmer. But I didn't know anything about the people of Knaan: most of them didn't even know each other because each one was living in their own world. How can you motivate people who have nothing to do? How can you help others feel happier if they are living in their fantasy world every day? How can you even read them if you can't access their world? I didn't think I could do any good as a storyteller, and I didn't have enough life experiences to share anyway. I was sure I could do more than just that.

Isaac left to do his job and I met with Doctor Manu, the city's senior engineer. He wore light blue overalls and had messy hair and a thick beard, like he hadn't showered for ages. He was cross-eyed and had a black semicircle beneath each eye. He looked like he had been looking at a computer screen his whole life. His assistant was a chubby girl with curly hair, who put me on a simulation bed and then stood next to a control panel attached to the bed while Doctor Manu walked around and checked stuff like a messy professor. He then started explaining.

"So I am actually excited to meet you."

"Can you talk slower?"

"Yes, I am sorry. Is this ok?"

"Yes."

I hated when they talked so fast. It reminded me how old I was, actually.

"I was told that a young defrosty had arrived, which is so rare here. You are the youngest to ever arrive."

"Nice to meet you," I said.

"This is an exciting time for us. You have a young mind. You experience the simulation different than us because you are not used to it. We can actually see the changes in your brain and how it is affected by the simulation, so we can make it better."

"What do you mean make it better?"

"Everything was initially programmed by humans, which means it had flaws and bugs. The system isn't perfect and is supposed to fix itself. But because it isn't human we have to balance it and check everything. To make sure it feels, looks, sounds, tastes and smells real."

"So you want me to be your guinea pig?"

I had to hear an honest answer.

"No, it's not like that at all. The simulation monitors everybody anyway. But if you would like to help us here in the lab, it would improve the simulation for everybody."

"Sure, I guess, I'll help. I have nothing better to do."

"Great, you are a game-changer. The team will be thrilled. Thank you."

"But I'm willing to participate only if you test me like the rest of the kids. I want to know if I fit into a different job. I don't want to be a storyteller."

He paused for a second. He was surprised to hear me bargain.

"Like I've told Padma, I don't mind having the test but I warn you that we never saw a defrosty succeed."

"I need to be tested for a role. Then you can run your tests."

"Sure, you are young, maybe you are different."

"So what is the test?"

"You won't notice it." He signaled to his assistant to start doing something and she began pushing some buttons behind my head. "This is happening on the back-end of your brain. We stimulate your brain with sensory information and test the response time and neural activity between the different parts of the brain. We also have your DNA sample."

"How does it tell you what I am good for?"

"If you're fast enough you can work in defense and security. If you have good motor skills you can be a technician, and if you have a strong logical side you can be an engineer."

"But I am not prepared for this."

"Like I said, it is all built upon your natural orientation. We do this test for kids when they are six years old to see what direction they are leaning toward, and teach them exactly that. Eventually the strong side will develop over the others and we test them again every year to make sure they are on the path to the right job."

"So you don't give them a choice."

"Choice is not needed because they will do what they excel at, and as such, will love it and be praised for it. We don't have enough jobs and places for people to experiment. Everything must be perfect for this city to survive."

"And what if it's not?"

"Then you do it for a few years as your mandatory service, and then leave the real world with the good feeling that you helped your friends and family to survive. You can be whatever you want in the simulation. But here, it has to be perfect."

"Ok, I'm ready."

"Just relax and stay still, although you can close your eyes or open them because that doesn't matter. It will only take a minute."

Doctor Manu and his assistant stepped away to watch the test on a screen on the wall. It was the most intense minute I had ever experienced. I don't think there is a drug in the world that could do the same as what happened to me there. I saw, heard, smelled, felt and tasted everything at once. It all happened so fast I couldn't understand what was happening. I saw lions running at me, cogs spinning, and waterfalls and geometric shapes. I saw neon colors and sunsets, snakes and trees. I heard Morse code and opera and whales and dolphins. I heard crickets and elephants, monkeys and bees. I felt metal on my hands and sand under my feet. Fire and ice. I tasted spicy and salty, sweet and sour. It all happened simultaneously. I kind of wished it to continue, but Dr. Manu came back and it was over. It wasn't pleasant at all but I actually felt every part of my body working and shooting electricity into my brain like I got hit by lightning. He then cut a hair from my head and gave it to his assistant to put into a different device. He looked at me and smiled. Then he looked at the device and stopped smiling.

"Oh, I am so sorry."

"What?"

"It seems like you are half-monkey, half-chimpanzee," and started laughing.

"It's just a joke I tell the kids to pass the time. I don't have the results yet."

What is it with doctors in this place?

The device beeped and his face went blank.

"What?"

"Uh, wait a minute."

It was nerve-wracking.

"Well, you don't fit any technical job here."

"What about security guard?"

"Your physical condition isn't—"

"—So there's nothing for me?"

"Your responses are slower than our minimum. The logic side of your brain isn't developed enough."

"But I was born three hundred years ago. This isn't fair."

"I am sorry but we can't risk having you in a technical or a security position. It will take you too many years to train and learn what children are learning from pretraining."

"Can't you put me in a special program?"

"We don't have those, unless you start basic training with the six-year-olds."

"I can't do that. What can I do?"

"Stay a storyteller, or a plumber, or a janitor. We need those desperately."

Wow, so many options…this place is just shitty. I didn't want to be frozen in the first place, nor did I want to be revived. Now they put me here and tell me to clean their toilets? No way, no way. There must be something else I can do.

"Thank you so much," I said, and left.

"What about laundry?" he shouted.

Coming from his mouth it almost sounded promising. Yeah, why not? Maybe I'll be a laundry technician. No, I want to be a detergent engineer or cleanliness scientist. How come in year 2321 there are still people who do these jobs? It's unbelievable. What happens if I don't get a job and President Padma decides to assimilate me?

I walked out of the lab and I thought I should start to get comfortable in this place without a guide, if I wanted to feel part of it. I needed to clear my mind of that last experience, anyway. I started walking clockwise next to the inner wall which meant that the curve was to the right behind me. I'm sure that people noticed I was a newbie. I wished I could go outside and run. That was usually what kept my temper down. It would release all my anger and I would come back exhausted and fueled with endorphins. The problem was that I couldn't go out because that could get me assimilated or shot at. I thought about the doctor who said, "Help us," on my first day, and how could I even help, and to whom. I just kept on walking and I came across a gym. I used to hate gyms. I hated running on a treadmill like a human version of a hamster wheel. I hated how everybody showed off their muscles and didn't wipe the sweat off the seats. But that's the only escape I had at the moment, and I had to run my anger off. *Stupid brain test.* I wasn't even aware of everything that happened at once. How could I succeed in something I had no control over? That was so unfair. I bet they did it at a young age to indoctrinate the children so they wouldn't rebel later. They probably told them how special and gifted they were so the kids thought they were the best.

The gym looked quite ordinary; white facilities, black weights. The treadmill was a little different, though. Above it was a helmet hanging from wires that ran from the ceiling. I put it on. It turned out to be a simulation helmet, which made me happy because I hated running and not seeing the view change. I could choose from several backgrounds like a desert, a jungle, a savanna and a snowy plain. I chose the savanna and started running. I didn't stretch or anything, nor did I care. The simulation was so real I forgot where I was for a second and panicked. I started running and the cool thing was that when I wanted the zebras to run with me, they immediately did. I started running faster. I left my zebra friends behind and got next to a cheetah that ran faster than me. I tried to catch it and felt my heart pumping fast. It felt good.

"*Want to race?*" I heard a voice ask me.

"*Hi, you want to race?*" it asked again.

I took the helmet off. Then I saw a boy younger than me with olive skin and short hair, running on a nearby treadmill.

"I am ok, thank you."

"*Why you talk so slow?*"

"Why you talk so fast?" I replied.

"I talk normal. So why not?"

"I was just defrosted. I can't compete."

"Are you the soldier?"

"What?"

I couldn't understand him, and I was panting from my run nonetheless.

"S-o-l-d-i-e-r?"

"Yes."

What a douche.

"Let's race. What are you afraid of?"

"Fine," I grunted.

He was so annoying that I didn't even care to lose as long as afterward he'd let me be. I admit, it was nice talking to someone new. So I put the helmet back on and saw him warming up next to me. I made him wear leopard skin and colored his face with warpaint just for fun. It made him look less annoying.

"Ok," he said. *"See the smoke?"*

"Yes."

I saw a smoke pillar in the distance. He must've created that himself.

"That's the finish line. Ready?"

"Yes."

A big red "3" appeared in front of my face. Then a "2" and a "1" and then a buzzing sound, and we started to run. He was fast but I knew I could keep up. I was already warmed up so I had the advantage. I opened a margin in front of him and felt the wind hitting my face. He smiled and looked forward like a hawk on a rabbit. Then he ran like hell. I was so surprised that I almost forgot to run. I had to pace up and try to reach him. I was three feet behind him, then four and five and six. By the time he got to the finish line I already gave up. My heart was racing and I was breathing heavily. My muscles were sore and I was sweating like a pig. I took the helmet off and I saw his stupid smile. It seemed like no effort for him.

"So that's the famous soldier."

"What are you talking about?"

"You don't look like a soldier and you don't run like one."

"Who do you think I am?"

"Everyone knows who you are. But I know you can't help us. Don't worry, soldier, next time you'll win, maybe."

"Help who, how?" I asked.

"*See you,*" he said, and left the gym.

"Wait, tell me how?" I tried to follow him, but I couldn't spot him in either direction.

I was confused and beaten by a teenage boy. That little prick. Maybe I was indeed too slow for this place.

Chapter 6

I came back to my room and went into the shower. I'd mastered the washing routine: ten seconds of water, followed by the soap spray, and then ten seconds of water to rinse it all out. Then air-dry with germs. It wasn't pleasant at all. Since I didn't yet know how to get a fresh pair of overalls I had to dry my sweaty one and wear them again.

I sat on my simulation bed and saw the other people in the room lying in their permanent state of assimilation. I assumed Isaac's wife was also among them. I couldn't see their faces under the bedcover but their body posture seemed calm. I wondered what might happen if he tried to open the bed and free her. It might be too traumatic for her. Who knows what life she had built for herself in there? Maybe she was young again and just started a whole new family. Maybe she lives in 21st-century Venice or Hawaii. Maybe she went back to her childhood home. It didn't sound so bad. It's better than being a plumber, a cleaner or even a storyteller. I had no stories in me anyway.

Oh wait. I have one. Don't die and go to the future. The climate is horrible and you'll be forced to live underground and clean toilets all day. How's that for a life lesson, kids?

Isaac came back looking for me. He studied my face and remained standing.

"Not what you hoped for?" he asked.

"No." I shrugged.

"What kind of 'No'?"

"I got nothing; I can't do anything in this place."

"Did he say why?"

"I am not fast enough and my logic isn't strong enough. So I am left with plumbing, cleaning and laundry. Which is, by the way, something you didn't explain to me, and now I'm sitting in my stinky overalls after running in the gym."

"You went to the gym?"

He raised his eyebrows.

"Yeah, why?"

"No one goes to the gym."

"So, you were about to explain laundry."

"Oh yes," he said, and pulled a drawer off the wall. He handed me clean overalls and I changed in the shower. I gave him the dirty one and he put it in another drawer.

"Anyway, you can still be a storyteller if you want."

"Or assimilate. President Padma has already presented me with that option."

"Yes, you were about to cross the line. It's good they caught you. You could have gone to trial for sneaking outside. Or worse, been hurt or killed."

"I was already killed, remember?"

He couldn't reply to that. It wasn't his fault and I **was** being nasty to him.

"I'm sorry, I know it's not your fault I'm here, I just have no one else to vent to."

"That's ok."

"They revived me in this concrete prison without me even wanting it, and then threaten to assimilate me if I escape. How do you keep sane around here?"

"You won't understand."

He wasn't impressed by my anger. And why would he? He's so wise and old, he's beyond anger.

"Tell me, because I sure need some sanity these days."

"It's an old Buddhist saying I tell myself every day."

"Buddhist? You?"

"After your time, when economies collapsed, more people started to get interested in that."

"So what do you say?"

He turned serious.

"Well?" I pressed him.

"I shall grow old, get sick and die. I can't escape aging, sickness and death. Everything I said or did is my sole responsibility. Everybody I know and cherish will fade away in time. Everything is connected. Everything changes. Control is an illusion."

I was overwhelmed.

"It's the most depressing saying I've ever heard."

"It's relieving if you think about it."

"I don't think so."

"Trust me, it works."

"You know, I just thought I'd grow up to do something more important. In the real world."

"This is the real world now and storytelling is important. You pass on knowledge and morals to the kids so when they grow up they don't screw everything up like we did."

"Stories didn't seem to help us not screw things up."

"Well, it's too late for us. But when these people will come out to the surface, they will be smarter."

"If they come out."

"Listen, you can go to pretraining or basic training and learn everything from the start. Then you can get retested ten years from now just to become somebody who sits in front of a computer all day and manages a quantum system. Sounds exciting, right?" he asked, sarcastically.

"But at least I'll be doing something that helps people, like security or technical stuff."

"I don't know what to tell you. Quantum computers or not, you'll be still sitting in front of a screen monitoring the systems like three hundred years ago. They don't let you monitor the systems from inside the simulation for obvious reasons."

I sighed. I felt like I was a burden on Isaac and this city because I didn't fit in. I had to be explained everything like a child. I wasn't even physically fit to be a guard.

"Anyway, I came here to tell you something else entirely."

"Now what?"

"President Padma wants to meet you. I think she has another job for you."

Excitement started tingling in my chest.

"Just ask yourself this," he added. "Do you want to directly affect people or do you want to affect the systems that affect people?"

Chapter 7

I sat in a waiting room outside the president's office. It was built inside the inner ring of the city. The waiting room was much nicer than the gray corridor. The concrete was painted white and had majestic looking illustrations on it. I sat there for quite awhile, while a security camera remained fixed on me. I assumed they had cameras to monitor everybody around the city. I bet if they detected anger in your simulation they would follow you outside to make sure you didn't act stupid.

A girl wearing yellow overalls came into the waiting room. She looked at the closed door and then at me. For a split second I swear she looked like Hadar, but then again I knew I couldn't yet fully trust my mind. She had brown hair that was held by a rubber band or some future thingy. She had a darker skin tone than me and light green eyes, high cheekbones and full lips. I didn't know why, but I started to get nervous.

"*Hi,*" she said, smiling.

"Hi," I said.

"*Are you here for the president?*"

"Yes, I have an appointment."

Appointment? She's not a doctor. Why was I nervous?

"*Cool.*"

"Can you talk slower? I am still not used to your speed."

"Oh..."

Her face lit up in the most beautiful way, like she was expecting to see me or something. I felt welcomed by her smile.

"...you are the soldier."

"Yes," I admitted.

She sent her hand for a shake and I shook her arm like Isaac taught me.

"What's your name?" she asked.

"Roy."

"Roy? I never heard that name before. Didn't they give you a new name?"

"Who was supposed to?"

"I don't know, someone who handles new names. Defrosties always have new names."

"Actually, I only met three people so far, not including the doctors."

"Ha, I heard about that. Was it scary at the beginning?"

"Yup."

"So, it's up to me to find you a new name," she said.

"I don't really want a new one."

"Don't worry, I'll find you a new one after I get to know you."

She wanted to get to know me?

"So how did it feel to die?"

Wow, that was blunt.

"I was frozen the whole time. I don't know."

"No, at the moment you were killed, how did it feel?"

She was so direct it made me uneasy. It was like she was interrogating me.

"I don't remember."

"Try."

"Why?"

"I am interested. I never asked a former soldier how it was to die."

"I don't want to remember that moment."

"Why, isn't it interesting?"

"I didn't want to die and if I remember it, it will hurt again."

"So? You're here now. It can't hurt you."

"It will because I lost family and friends…"

"Then I will be your friend, is that ok?"

"Well, yeah. You didn't tell me your name."

"It's Shanta."

"Shanta, like Shanti?"

"Quite similar, have you heard it before?"

"I just know the word."

"It means 'Peaceful.' What does 'Roy' mean?"

"It's a biblical name, meaning 'My Shepherd'."

She started giggling.

"Shepherd? Like sheep? Who is your Shepherd?"

"God, I guess."

She giggled more.

"Why are you laughing?"

"I imagine God is holding you on a leash, shepherding you while you eat grass."

"That's not what a shepherd does. Didn't they teach you that in school?"

"They teach us about climate and technology and ethics and whatever we need to survive. Not about old-time name meanings."

"You don't study the bible?"

She giggled again.

"We do, we study that religions helped to destroy the world."

"I thought it was pollution and heat."

"Yeah, but religions made people blind to the truth."

I didn't know what to say about that. It wasn't a time for a debate.

The door opened and two guards with dark blue overalls came out and greeted Shanta. The president then came out.

"Mom, the soldier is here to see you," she said.

'Mom'??? I just had a talk with the president's daughter and made a total fool out of myself?

"Again, nice to meet you, Roy."

"Nice to meet you."

We shook arms and she was pleasant.

"So I see that you already met Shanta. Do you mind if she comes in with us? I invited her to get to know you."

So it wasn't a coincidence: she was here, and so friendly.

"Sure."

We all went inside and sat on little couches that looked like they were made of thick, plastic-like fabric. There were four screens on the wall displaying different graphs and numbers. On the other side of the room was a window that showed a view of the coastline.

"This is…normal," I said, pointing around the room.

"I try to keep my room as simple as I can so I can concentrate."

"Is that a real window?"

"No that's just a screen showing me the view from any security camera I choose. I like to be reminded of the outside."

"Nice."

"So let's start anew, shall we? Tell me a little bit about yourself."

"I don't know where to start."

"Anywhere will be fine."

"So my name is Roy, but Shanta told me that I need to get a new name. I am 19, or 319, depending on how you calculate it."

They giggled a bit, though it was an awful corny joke they've must have heard a thousand times from people like me.

"I was born in Tel Aviv and you know, I feel that if I start talking about my past I'll just start crying again so I'd rather not."

"That's understood. Let me tell you a little bit about myself and this place. I've been President of Knaan for over twenty years now. This place is a miracle. Everything here is designed to be self-sustainable until we can go back to living outside. But this sustainability is delicate. Everything has a part to play. For example, there mustn't be violence and friction between people. Also, there mustn't be an overconsumption of resources. That's why everything is regulated and automated by our systems."

"I see."

"Like I said yesterday, I consider all residents my own children. So the most important thing I can say to you is try to fit in as well as you can. Find your place and play along with others. If you get that, you'll feel at home again and everything will be just wonderful for you."

She looked at Shanta and smiled. "That's why I asked Shanta to guide you and welcome you."

But how do I make her like me for real?

"Thank you, I intend to do the best I can to find my place. But when I went to get tested—"

"—Say no more. Another reason I invited you here was to offer you a special job only a few can do. I feel that this might be something you will be perfect for."

No laundry? No toilets? No way!

"What is it?"

"We have an intelligent security system that operates automatically on the outside. But, like any other system, sometimes it experiences malfunctions and erosion. I'm offering you an important role in being a Gun Tech Assistant, which means retrieving broken guns from the outside and installing the fixed ones."

I almost shouted, '*Hell yeah!*'

"Is that what happened before?"

"Those guards worked outside the safe zone to maintain our water pumps. You'll be only working within the gun circle, so you'll be covered by our systems. Nothing has happened to a GTA within twenty years of my service."

I wasn't pleased with unnecessary danger after already dying once, but it wasn't new to me either. On the other hand, it was an important job. Plus I would get to see the outside world, like I wanted.

"GTAs mostly go out at night. We have special suits for protection just like you saw. You will learn how to dismount the guns quickly so the rest can be done inside. You are the most highly trained person here in combat and stressful conditions. This job is perfect for you, and I'm sure you're curious about the outside like most defrosties are."

"What about the 'Purists'?"

She paused for a second to think.

"Like I said, you will wear a special suit and our security system will be running at all times to keep you safe. I'm not saying you'll be out there every night, but whenever the security of this city is in jeopardy, you'll be expected to quickly get us back to full capacity. This job can save a lot of lives, Roy."

I looked at Shanta, and she was smiling like she was excited for my new role. It got me excited, as well. I could be someone that people needed here, and I'd get to go outside while no one else could.

"Do you know what our most precious resource is?"

"Water?" I immediately answered.

"Think harder."

"Electricity?"

"Security. It's security that keeps all the systems running and it keeps people relaxed and happy. We feel secure if everything goes according to plan and expectations. People need to know that they are safe, and it's better if they even forget about it. That's how we can achieve less stress, less fighting, fewer unpleasant events. Think about your job as maintaining order and sanity by providing security."

I wasn't really debating; I knew I had to take it.

"I agree," I said with pride. "Thank you."

"Thank you, Roy, for choosing to be a part of this miraculous city," she said, shaking my arm gently. "Don't hesitate to come to me with anything that bothers you. I consider you one of my children."

"Thank you so much. I hoped I didn't have to be a storyteller."

"We were all surprised to see a nineteen-year-old coming off the ice. It took us a day, but we found you a more suitable job. Don't pay attention to that test. It was a horrible idea to begin with for a defrosty."

"Can I ask you for something?"

"Sure."

"Could you check what happened to my parents? Doctor Ashish told me there might be information in the other cities but he couldn't determine their status."

"Yes, I'll check with him immediately."

Chapter 8

In the middle of the night I woke up to pee, but couldn't go back to sleep because I started to miss Hadar. Missing her used to catch me in the throat every couple of days in my previous life, and now I thought about her because she resembled Shanta. Or Shanta resembled her. First I thought about bringing Hadar in the simulation, but then I had a better idea. I had to find Shanta again and discover what she was like without her mom watching. So that was the first thing I'd do that morning, before I had to start my Gun Technician Assistant training.

So I woke up Isaac.

"How do I find someone in the city?"

"It's too early."

"Please."

He was stretching in bed. I could hear his old bones creak.

"Do you know who they are, or are you guessing?"

"I know."

"Just think about them and try to contact them inside," he said, yawning and turning in bed.

"How will I know I am talking to the real her and not my imagination her?"

"Oh, so it's a 'her,' eh?" That seemed to grab his awareness.

"Don't get annoying."

"Is she pretty?"

I paused.

"Well?"

I guess he wasn't completely in my favor after I took the new job.

"Just see if it lets you contact her or not. This whole thing is so intuitive and you keep asking me questions instead of trying for yourself. My story ended, like all stories should. It's time for you to play alone."

"Ok, fine."

"Will they defrost another one to replace you?"

"I don't know yet."

I could see how disappointed in me he was, but he was right: maybe I should have started to be more independent. I lay inside the simulation bed and imagined I was in the main street. Everyone passed me by very quickly as I was looking for Shanta. I got a message appearing in front of my eyes saying she was not available for calls and that I should leave a message. At least I knew it was real, otherwise I would have just been able to summon her. I said something like, *'Hi, it was nice to meet you yesterday, and I'm wondering if we can meet again today?'* I didn't know what else to say to convince her to see me because I didn't know anything about her. I left the simulation.

To get to the training I had to remember the way that led to the corridor inside the inner circle of the city. I was already late. I tried to ask people where to go. It took me four attempts to talk at the right speed for them to understand me and for me to understand them. Eventually, I went back a hundred meters and pushed a door. From there I had to climb two floors up a staircase. The air felt warmer, like I was actually closer to the surface. If I could feel the heat underground, it meant that it was burning outside. I hoped we weren't going to train out there in the middle of the day, despite wanting to go out and see things for what they were.

The corridor was empty, and it wasn't as sexy as the main street. It was dirty and darker, like a backstage or a service corridor. I followed noises to another room. I knocked.

"Come *in*," a woman's voice shouted back at me.

She was chubby compared to the others I'd met, although she was more tanned. She had grease and dust smeared all over her hands and face.

She cleaned her hands with a dirty towel and shook my arm.

"I'm Viti, you must be Roy."

My face twitched, which is what happens when somebody talks fast to me and I concentrate on what they are saying.

"Sorry, I should talk slower."

The room was full with tools, spare parts on shelves, and a big gun lying on the table in the middle of the room. It was like nothing I'd ever seen before.

"Nice to meet you," I said. "Are you alone here?"

"Yes, you're looking at the only gun technician of the city."

"Just one?"

"Well, as you can see, it's not so glamorous a job, yet an important one."

"I thought I'd see a whole team."

"I don't need a team. The systems take care of the actual threats. I just fix the guns from time to time, and they are pretty reliable."

"But Padma made it sound like it was so…"

"Yes, she knows how to talk, doesn't she? The former gun techs are still lying around in the city in case we need them and soon someone will replace me." She smiled and touched her round belly. "But as long as I'm here, you'll be working with me."

"Congratulations."

"Thanks, hope you're a fast learner."

"I used to be."

"Don't worry about it. As long as you follow the rules you'll be fine."

"What are the rules?"

"We'll get to them. First, come meet your new best friend."

She approached the gun on the table and I followed her.

"Lift it, it's not that heavy."

I held it for a second but had to put it down. I wasn't in great shape.

"Hey! Easy. I just finished fixing it. You need to hit the gym more often, apparently."

"I just woke up two days ago."

"Right, but you probably know about guns."

"Not this kind."

"Good point. This, my friend, is a laser gun." She stroked it like you pat a dog.

"Cool."

"Huh?"

"I mean, awesome."

"There's nothing cool about it, it's freaking hot as hell, and that's the point."

"How does it work?"

"Short version? Energy is built into a capacitor that starts the chain reaction for the laser to light. When it reaches the right amount of energy, the shot is released. Since the light wavelength is so coherent there's no diffusion, so this thing can burn a hole through your chest."

"What about dust?"

"We got ourselves an intelligent creature here. Dust is the enemy, as much as I try to keep this baby sealed and greased, dust will interfere with the lens and cause the electric circuit to heat and burn itself. That's why you're going to learn how to help me fix this baby."

I was surprised to see it wasn't so complicated. And as futuristic as it was, I could see the paint fading, scratch marks all over it, and loose wires. Everything was designed to be replaced by spare chips, electric parts and whole circuit boards. The important task was to be able to repair the little parts ourselves without replacing the whole card, because spare parts were available, but not unlimited. It was our job to replace them according to the right schedule and not because we arbitrarily wanted to. We had a special device to examine that and keep track of maintenance.

It took me about three hours to learn the basics and go over the tools and parts. I could use the screen to learn more.

I was thirsty and hungry and I needed a break.

"Do you have a simulation bed here?"

"No, why? Did I bore you that much?"

"I'm just hungry."

"Oh I don't eat in the simulation no more; my room is too far away."

"So what do you do?"

"I just eat the actual stuff."

"The actual bug juice?"

She started laughing. "Yeah, if you call it like that. Come, I'll show you. We're getting hungry ourselves." She patted her belly.

I was hesitant, but she had been nice to me and got me curious. I followed her into the corridor and another level down, where it was cooler. We went inside a much bigger room. It was a hall filled with big metal containers and pipes. It was noisy, like a million bug legs moving and rubbing against each other, which is what the noise actually was. They were jammed into metal containers and just procreated while fighting over food. The food technician explained how they lived inside the container in complete darkness and fed on tempered human waste, algae and other nutrients they vacuum out of the sea. When the mass is critical they let a certain amount of bugs out by showing them the light to a different container. The second container zaps the whole bunch with an electric shock. The bugs fall to the floor and get sucked into the third container, where they're ground up and mixed with water and more algae. I had to vomit, and I did, on the floor.

I told her I'd be back later and she shouted to come back before sunset so she could take me outside, to the actual surface. So I was disgusted and happy at the same time. I didn't know what to do with myself. I wanted to learn everything about those guns, but the sight of the bug juice factory was horrible. And that's the stuff I had to eat for the rest of my life, apparently. I ran in the middle of the street straight to my room, and into my bed. Isaac was there and I didn't even say hello. I just dipped inside the simulation and went to the beach.

The simulation bed became humid because I was breathing so heavily under the cover, but I didn't care. I made myself a cold mango shake and drank it like a dehydrated dog. Then I made myself a pineapple shake. I didn't want to eat something that belonged to that processed monstrosity. After being able to relax a little bit I noticed a flashing red dot in the corner of my sight. It was a message from

Shanta, to meet her at 21:00 at a festival inside the simulation. No "See you there," no "I'll be expecting you," no "Loved it if you'd come and meet," just the necessary information. I thought her voice sounded like she was smiling, though. I didn't know what to do to pass the time until sunset so I just went to sleep.

When I woke up I went back to the gunroom with an uneasy feeling in my stomach. The main street ceiling light had changed its color according to the sunset outside, at least that's what it looked like, and was nice. So I took my time getting to the gunroom. Viti was waiting for me when I entered the room.

"I don't know, maybe you'd prefer to be a cleaner. I could use a cleaner here."

"Sorry I'm late."

"Listen, buddy, this is no game. This is not 'The Future Show.' This is life now, ok? You have to respect the rules."

"You told me to forget the rules for now."

The lights dimmed and flickered for a few moments. Viti smiled as if she saw fireworks over the city on Independence Day.

"My babies are working," she said with pride.

"The Purists again?"

"No, neighbors trying to ask for milk. Of course it's the Purists."

"Why don't they stop when one of theirs dies?"

"Every stupid one thinks he'll break our systems. It turns out that men aren't so smart. They never were, actually."

"MEN were smart enough to build this place to protect us."

"But not smart enough to keep the whole world from collapsing."

She had a point.

"So why do the Purists do it?"

"For everyone dead there are some others watching and studying our system. But they can't break it."

"How can you be so sure?"

"The fact is they never succeeded."

"It doesn't sound like a good enough answer."

"When they study us, our systems study them, and we're faster."

"So what's next?" I asked.

"We put on a Cactus, follow me."

She pushed the tray with the gun out of the room and I followed her till we reached an elevator.

"Are we going out now?"

"You betcha."

I started to get excited and my stomach tingled. The tip of my fingers felt electrified. We got into an elevator and went one floor up, where the air was warmer. I started to perspire. I could hear a muffled hum that was coming from the surface so I figured we were just a few meters below the surface. She pushed the tray into the room and onto another platform elevator. It was lit with red light, like a photography dark room. By the side of it was a metal cabinet. She opened it, and there were four guns and four of the spiky suits that I saw the guards wear to go outside.

She took one of them out.

"This is the Cactus suit. It's a camouflage suit that muffles sounds and deflects your figure. It also absorbs the environment temperature so you'll be invisible to infrared. Oh, and it also diffuses radars."

"It didn't help those guards who got shot two days ago."

"Those idiots never follow procedures."

"Did the Purists ever try to attack you while you were out there?"

"Oh, usually I don't go out myself, that's your job."

"But…"

"You're the GTA, I do the technical part, and you do the dangerous part. I'll go out with you just for a few times."

She handed me a suit and it stung my hand. I put the pants on first, then the vest. Then I had to attach the sleeves, and lastly the headpiece. Just like I saw the guards do. For all of its technological sophistication, it wasn't easy to put on or move in; walking too fast or making too sharp a movement caused you to get stung by a metal fibers. That's why they called it the Cactus. Then she handed me a gun.

"Instead of using gunpowder that you're familiar with, these guns use a strong, repulsive magnetic field to shoot. The little glowing bar represents the power left in the battery. And the bullets are pretty standard; besides that they can be shot to a longer range than old, regular bullets."

The gun felt powerful in my hand. I looked between the cross hairs and got the sense of it by moving around a bit, assuming fire position and aiming. Just like the old times, two days ago.

"I'm going to show you what do to and you're just going to shut up and watch me."

"Got it."

She got dressed and we moved slowly toward the platform elevator with the gun on the tray. It was extremely annoying to move in that thing. I had to spread my legs a little bit and lift my arms to the sides to avoid chafing myself. It felt heavy and clumsy, not like a battle suit at all. But if it was as sophisticated as she said it was, I guess a couple of stings were worth saving my life.

"First rule: you don't go out without permission. Repeat that."

"I do not go out without permission."

"Second rule: you stay out as briefly as you need."

"I stay out as briefly as I need."

"You only go out after the sunset."

"Do I need to repeat everything?"

"Repeat."

"I only go out after sunset."

"You breathe through your nose and blink a lot."

"Why?"

"Because it's the hottest, most humid place you'll ever be and it burns to breathe. Also, never pick the same elevator twice and don't create a pattern."

"Never create a pattern?"

"Good."

The two of us stood on the platform. It was camouflaged with actual rocks and sand. She leaned over to get her eyes scanned, and then pressed a button on the intercom.

"This is Viti and frosty coming up for a switch."

A male voice answered.

"Scan his eyes please," the voice said.

"You need to stand here." She pointed at the place she was standing. I took off my headpiece and got my eyes scanned.

"Good luck," the man said.

The elevator started to rise and the red light dimmed.

"One last thing," she whispered. "I'm not your tour guide, so look at the view but ask me nothing."

The opening above us dilated and I could see the sky for the first time. It was radiating a majestic red, pink and purple. Like nothing I'd seen before. I didn't know it was pollution that made the light break that way. We walked out of the platform onto a dry piece of land with rocks scattered all over the place.

And then I saw it. It was just as Isaac has showed me on my first day. I was standing in a circle of gray-colored poles that was surrounded by a high fence. You could see the erosion marks on the poles from withstanding the heat and sandblasts. Each pole had four laser guns at different heights facing each direction, constantly panning left and right with an irritating rusty sound. Two cameras sat atop each tower, one facing inward and one outward. A Zeppelin balloon was connected by a wire above each tower, with a wind turbine inside it. I couldn't say how big the circle of poles was, but it was huge. Inside sat hundreds of solar panels, all facing the sunlight at the same angle. Some had cracks and some were totally shattered.

The air was extremely humid. Sweat was dripping into my eyes forcing me to blink every few seconds. I breathed through my nose and was sweating like a racehorse. Hot wind was blowing from the west, shooting sand through the air. There were no trees. I could hear no sound other than the humming of the A/C units and the turbines above us. I could have marveled more, but Viti had rushed me, causing me to get stung by the Cactus suit. I started to bleed. She shouted that I would get used to it.

"Are you sure you're supposed to do this while you're pregnant?"

"See anyone else here?"

After we reached the closest tower she approached a metal box and opened it with a key. One of the guns lowered when she turned it to the left. She replaced it by opening the harness that held it to the tower. It didn't seem difficult at all.

"Wait till one of these puppies breaks and you have to climb up there yourself to open the harness."

I started to have trouble breathing, as if the sand was filling my lungs. My eyes were stinging so badly that I could barely keep them open, and I almost tripped on a rock when I tried to turn around and go back inside. I tried to see if I could spot any buildings on the coastline where Tel Aviv used to be, but I got a sandblast to the mask. It felt good to be outside, but not physically. It was like a boot camp in hell. I wanted to drink so badly and breathe clean air. Yet I felt like I accomplished something.

Then Viti collapsed on the ground and started shouting and breathing fast.

"What happened?"

"…Contractions…I'm not supposed…"

"What's wrong with the baby?" I asked.

"Take me inside…idiot!"

She was screaming so loud I wondered if anyone could hear us. I tried to carry her by the armpits.

"Watch it!" she screamed.

I dragged her on the ground. She was heavy, and screaming and getting scoured by the Cactus suit. She didn't deserve this.

"Get me to the clinic!"

At least she had mounted the gun already.

I managed to drag her to the platform and it automatically lowered us. A medical team was waiting with a stretcher on wheels. I guess they saw us on camera. They put her there without removing the Cactus suit.

My lungs hurt. I was bleeding beneath my suit. Rough start.

Chapter 9

When I got to the clinic, Dr. Manu was there talking to Viti and her husband.

"Thank you, frosty."

She held my hand and started crying.

"I almost lost him."

"You'll be fine," her husband said. "Everything will be just fine." He then thanked me, too.

"I spoke with President Padma. They're going to find someone else to train you in the meanwhile," Viti said.

Manu was smiling at me in a suspicious way.

"So, I hear you got a job."

"I did," I said with confidence.

"Good for you. At least you have your luck."

He had lost his guinea pig.

"Sorry I was being a little rough on you," Viti said.

"That's ok," I replied.

She wasn't that bad, actually. I had it worse during the Army training. Way worse.

"I can do it myself."

I looked Manu right in his puffy eyes.

"Gun tech, you alone?" He laughed at my face.

"Yes. Diagnosing malfunctions is automated anyway. I'm more capable of going outside alone than anyone."

"A dangerous proposal from someone who was found unqualified for technical positions," he said, and looked at Viti, who shrugged. She was too tired to care.

"Talk to the president. I bet she'll say yes."

"I doubt that."

Manu looked at Viti for approval again, like I was crazy. And I was but I wanted to get back at him. The chances of me becoming a full-time technician were zero but I had nothing to lose. Plus I hated him.

"He's a fast learner," she said. "All the information is in the computer anyway. And I can guide him through here for awhile."

"You're both crazy, I won't allow it. The former gun tech will replace you until you feel better or the new one takes the job. And you..." He looked at me. "You're just the GTA and that's lucky enough."

"This just made me want to talk to President Padma myself. See you soon," I said with a fake confident smile.

I left the clinic proud of myself. If I wanted to blend in I'd have to earn their respect. I must believe in myself first. And I think I just started to no matter what happens.

Before my date with Shanta I just walked around in circles in the main street looking at people. I had to give myself something to do or else I'd go crazy waiting. I tried to make the best of the situation and to progress my current status. But in most cases you just have to wait for a reaction or a change, because it's not up to you. So I waited for Shanta.

She had told me to meet her at a festival in the simulation, but I didn't know what that meant. I hoped it was a type of a date. Since we'd be meeting in a simulation, showering in the real world didn't matter, nor did changing my clothes. Since I couldn't bring myself to eat after what I saw in the roach factory, my stomach growled and demanded attention. I tried to pace myself so when I'd finish circling the city I'd end up back in my room. It was five minutes before our date and I started to walk fast and funny like those competitive walkers at the Olympics.

I went inside the simulation and was automatically transferred to a grassy plain in the mountains. The sun was shining but it wasn't hot. So many people were there, all dressed in their white overalls. Dance music was playing. I can't explain what it sounded like, but it was fast and people were dancing funny. There was a big stage and behind it a colorful sign read *Holi Festival 2321*. President Padma went onstage and the music was turned down. 'Her Children' hailed her. Why would they ever leave this place in favor of the surface when they could live here for free and always get what they want? Padma spoke about how many children were born this year and how efficient the systems became. About senior students who moved to their next role in the city. And then, surprisingly, she was speaking about me. Out of ten thousand people who were there, she chose to talk about me, the newbie.

"As you all know, we unfreeze a new storyteller every once in awhile, so we can pass on the knowledge about the old world and learn the morals of the previous generations. But this time we didn't welcome another grandpa, to our surprise."

The whole crowd was laughing because she was charismatic and down-to-earth. She was a real leader and they loved her.

"The new citizen is actually here among us. Roy, could you come onstage?"

I was blushing. I didn't know why, I have never blushed. By now all virtual eyes were on me as I walked through the crowd to the stage. I climbed the stairs and she opened her arms for a hug. We hugged for a second and I saw how massive the crowd was; young and old, short and tall, women and men.

"Roy is only nineteen and has a bright future in New Knaan. He shows great potential. He is the only person in this city that was actually a trained combat soldier."

"I present you Roy, our new Gun Tech Assistant!"

The crowd exploded. I felt loved and appreciated although I hadn't done anything yet. This place was becoming my home more and more.

Padma then took some yellow powder from a bucket near her feet. She clenched her fist and presented it to the crowd. She said something in a language I couldn't understand and then threw the powder in the air. It shimmered in the sunlight. People were ecstatic and started throwing colorful powder at each other. The air filled with clouds of various colors, staining their white overalls. They came here to dirty themselves? What was that? Breaking the routine kind of thing? At the time, I didn't know it was a Hindu tradition that symbolized the beginning of spring and the victory of good over evil.

As I walked down from the stage I saw Shanta. She was there, all relaxed and colorful. She looked so beautiful.

"Hi, nice to see you again." She shook my arm.

"You, too," I said.

"Are you excited?"

"Are you?"

"*Yes*," she answered with a big smile, "*I am going to show you some neat stuff.* Sorry," she said slowly. "Show you some neat stuff."

She turned away from the crowd and I followed her. While we were walking on the green plain I felt better and better; me, a defrosty, on a date with the president's daughter.

"I was outside today," I said.

"Wow, how was it?"

"It's hard to breathe. Sand blows in your face. It's hot, and the Cactus suit is painful…"

"But it's real."

"Yes, but this is real also," I said.

"I mean, as opposed to this simulation."

"Yes, but you know, you can't compare the two becau—"

"—Can I show you something?" she asked with excitement.

"Sure."

I soon found myself on a white, tropical beach wearing a tee shirt and shorts. Shanta stood next to me wearing a Hawaiian-looking grass dress. We were standing on the sand but it was elevated; we were on a giant sandcastle.

"Did you build this?"

She nodded her head and smiled.

"This is awesome."

"You want awesome? Wait till you see this."

A blink after and we were standing on top of an orca whale, riding on its back while it was swimming against the waves. Shanta was holding onto a leash that was connected to its head. I held her waist. I felt the rubbery whale's skin under my feet. Salt water splashed in my eyes each time the whale leaped over another wave. I felt Shanta's waist bones and the soft skin around them. She looked back at me and smiled. The sun lit up her eyes and a wet lock of hair rested on her face.

"This is what you do every day?" I shouted.

"Sometimes," she smiled. "Sometimes I do this—"

She pointed upwards.

I heard a screech in the sky. I tried to see where it came from but the sun was in my eyes. Out of nowhere a figure blocked the sun, becoming bigger until I could see it. It was a dragon. It reached down with both its legs and caught us. I was scared, even though I knew everything I experienced was part of the simulation. The dragon held us gently and flew away. I saw the orca diving in the sea beneath us as we rose higher and further away. The wind was blowing in my face. I looked at her, smiling.

"This is so fun!" I shouted.

"Yes, but don't you notice something?"

"Like what?" Everything was perfect.

The dragon started to descend quickly into what seemed like a jungle. My stomach was in my throat, though I knew I was physically in my bed. It felt so real and so scary.

"Can you slow down?" I asked.

"Too fast for you?"

The dragon started to swirl in the air like a corkscrew, descending even faster. I started to get dizzy. I closed my eyes and told myself it wasn't real, yet I could still feel the pull of gravity and the wind in my face.

"Don't wake up, you sissy." She held onto me.

"Just stop it. It's not fun anymore."

In a second, the dragon had let go and dropped us from the sky.

"You asked for it!" she shouted during the free fall.

I screamed. I'm not ashamed to say it, but I screamed like a little girl. Even though I knew it wasn't real, when a dragon drops you over a jungle you are allowed to shit your pants. We landed inside a big, blue lake surrounded by the jungle. The water was so clear. I opened my eyes to see Shanta swimming up with me. We both reached the surface of the water at the same time, breathing and smiling.

"We couldn't actually drown if I stayed under, right?"

"Of course not, it's a simulation, dummy."

"I know, I know, just thinking aloud."

"So you don't notice anything weird?"

We started swimming back to shore.

"Like riding on a whale and flying with a dragon?"

"No, I mean that there's no one here but us."

"Oh. What's so weird about it? It's your world."

We sat on the sand, by the water. I decided I didn't want my clothes to feel wet so I turned them dry in my mind.

"It can get lonely here sometimes."

"But you can invite other people to share your simulation, can't you? Like you just did with me."

"Yes, but people are not like that. Everyone has their own little fantasy world, which is perfect for their taste. They set the rules and the atmosphere. Now, why would you let anyone else decide what your simulation looks like if you can control it by yourself? You can always get what you want. The constant pleasure directly to your brain is addictive. You don't know fear, loss, or anxiety. Everything is open and bright, not like Knaan's concrete walls. You might think it gets boring after awhile but it actually gets more and more fun. As long as you immerse yourself and forget about the physical world, you reach new extremes. You get addicted to them, despite never being able to truly share the same experience with another person."

"What if people do get lonely?"

"They create companions, like I have a whale and a dragon. Doesn't have to be human, right?"

"And you're trying to say that all this amazing experience is bad?"

"Not bad, but lonely, not human, not organic. People who don't speak to someone in reality for so long become less human. They become like addicted babies."

"But isn't it better than living inside concrete walls only? How do you keep everyone sane?"

"Let me tell you about 'sanity.' It starts when you're a baby. You're put in the simulation after only three months. You can't control anything because you're still a baby. Your parents don't have to touch you or play with you physically. Everything is done by using the simulation. And if they have to work, you're left with a virtual nanny. During twelve years of school you're taught in a virtual class along with other real people. You're not obliged to meet them outside. Whenever you get time alone you dive in by yourself. Some play together, but generally when people become older, they become more different and independent. You don't need friends or parents to help you fulfill your wishes. You can do anything by yourself in the simulation and it becomes addictive. When your service to the city is done there's nothing else to do around but stay inside 24/7 in a magnificent, self-centered fantasy world. Why would anyone go out?"

"But I've seen people out."

"That's just a tiny percent of the actual population."

"But it also keeps the security, like your mother said."

"There was a power outage, I was six maybe. I finished school and I was playing with my pony-unicorn. Not only did the simulation stop, but also the main street was in complete darkness. So did the air conditioning. It was hard to breathe. I wanted my mommy but she was working, and since I was only six, I didn't remember how to get to her office. I was afraid. It was so dark and people were shouting and making scary voices. That day I understood how fragile this city is. I couldn't trust it anymore. We're so dependent on our systems that at any minute this city could become a death trap, because we're so wrapped up in each of our own fantasy worlds that we don't know how to interact and solve real world problems."

"You don't sound like the president's daughter when you speak like that."

"She doesn't know I speak like that."

"What about your father?"

"Nobody knows, probably dead."

"What happened?"

"When I was four he was sent to help the southern city."

"Sent outside?"

"Yes. He was one of the senior engineers, and the city in the south couldn't repair their security systems. So he went out, though never got there."

"I'm sorry."

"That's ok. I don't remember much of him."

"Still, the city is safer than the outside."

"But for how long?"

"Does your mother know what you feel?"

"Of course not, that would ultimately screw her up."

I sighed deeply. I got myself between the daughter and the mom.

"Let's go out," she said, "I want to show you something else."

"As long as you don't plan more free falls."

I moved my butt closer to her and leaned over to try and kiss her. She immediately stood up and looked at me in a serious face. Was I wrong to try? Maybe there are different customs for that here.

"Do you trust me?" she asked.

"Sure…" I said.

"Don't hesitate. Do you trust me?"

"Yes."

"I trust you, Roy."

"Well, great." I was surprised to hear that, knowing I didn't do anything to deserve it.

"Then let's wake up. Meet me next to the gym in two minutes."

I awoke in my bed. The main street was darker. The light from above was bluish and resembled the light from a full moon, which I guess was the case above ground. I hurried to the gym where she was waiting for me. I could sense she wasn't the same. She was serious. My heart was pounding; I didn't know what do to. Was this still a date? Am I to be more assertive or just go along with her? I didn't know if she was trying to impress me or boss me around. I didn't like not being in control but it's not like I could pick her up in my parents' car and go to the movies.

She walked in front of me. I kept pace behind her, breathing her air, smelling her true fragrance. We turned right into the inner circle of the city. Then we started hearing gunshots from within the inner circle corridors. She was looking at me with fear in her eyes. The loud bursts were getting closer and closer. We already pivoted towards the exit when I looked back and saw two of Knaan's guards falling dead right in behind us.

"What do we do?" she asked.

"Stay here."

Instinctively my eyes fell to a fallen guards' gun. I slid on the floor and stopped right before I reached the corner of the corridor. Then I crawled and grabbed a gun. In that moment the wall exploded next to me. Bullets ricocheted. I hid behind the wall and took a quick look at the gun, it looked like the one Viti gave me, and the basic mechanism looked familiar. It had more electronics and LEDs. Shots ricocheted off the wall again. Shanta was no longer there.

I had to time myself right. I thought I heard footsteps or something pounding against the floor. I took off my shoe and threw it behind the corner.

Immediately shots were fired on it, and my shoe was riddled. I leaped around the corner and shot a soldier twice in the chest and once in the head. He was wearing a green IDF uniform. What?

I woke up in my room again in a state of hyperventilation. Shanta was there holding my shoulder.

"It's ok," she smiled, "I just had to know I could trust you."

"What just happened?"

"You were still at the simulation."

"How did you do that?"

"Come with me, I'll explain everything."

She led me down the stairs and through a series of small, dark corridors. This time it was real and you could almost taste the mold and rust smells in the air. I didn't remember how to retrace the route in my head. The air was dense, heavier, and warmer. There was noise coming from within the walls, and it sounded like the repetitive growl of an engine or a turbine. I wished she would take me to her private hangout place. I was nervous and excited at the same time. Will she kiss me here? Will she do more? She went into a dark room and pulled me inside. The door was shut behind me. We weren't alone anymore.

"Roy, meet the resistance. *Guys, this is Roy.*"

This wasn't a date, this was a trap. I took the bait and got pulled into the belly of the beast. I couldn't stay there; I was supposed to be in training tomorrow to do the best to blend in. I couldn't fall for the only girl who was dangerous to me.

There were three others beside Shanta, looking at me with disgust and resentment: the kid from the gym, who was standing next to Shanta, holding her hand. Was she with that asswipe? Next to them was the short girl with curly black hair from Dr. Manu's lab, wearing orange overalls. Then there was the ponytail doctor who gave me the shot on the first day.

Shanta turned to them and spoke.

"*Roy is just out of the oven, and as you know he used to be a combat soldier, trained in all sorts of field warfare. But now, this is the best part, he got a job as the gun tech assistant.*"

She looked at me and said, "*With a little help from my mom.*"

Everyone started to laugh and clap. Shanta was pleased. She made her mom help the resistance without realizing it.

"He will help us prevent the invasion."

"What? No, I will not. What the hell is this?" I interrupted her.

The boy from the gym stepped in and pushed me against the door.

"You don't speak like that to her, got it?"

My instincts kicked in and I grabbed this collar and his chin before I could even notice what I was doing. Shanta laid a hand on my shoulder. I released my grip.

"I'm not helping you, I have a job here."

Everyone was looking at Shanta, who looked distressed. I wanted to go easy on her, but I was not going to be pushed around and tricked by a bunch of kids. Let alone fight for them.

"Roy, you've been outside. You've seen the rust, the decay of the systems, and you've seen how addictive the simulation can be."

"I've seen nothing, just heard the stories that you've told me. From what I know, this place is the safest, happiest place on earth."

"The Purists have tried to invade us in the past. They will again, and it's just a matter of time until they find a weak spot. Guess what will they find when they go inside? Thousands of innocent sleeping people who don't know how to defend themselves. It's going to be a massacre."

"We have guns," I stated.

The ponytail doctor interrupted. "How many are actually working? Do you know? And how many guards do we have?"

"We have enough, probably."

Shanta cut in again. "Do you know why my mother had agreed to give you this job? It's not because you're bravest and fittest. It's because you're expendable."

I didn't see that coming.

She continued. "Sure, you have more skills to survive out there, but if something should happen to you, nobody would care."

"What do you know about fighting?" I asked them while scanning their eyes with my gaze.

The gym boy got closer to me again. "*Shut up now, we heard enough from you.*"

He turned to Shanta. *"I told you he wasn't good from the first day I met him. He's weak, he's not native, and he doesn't care. He's an old man in a young's man body."*

"We all agreed he's our only chance, we need him on our side."

"Well, he doesn't want to. So now what? He'll just go back and snitch."

"He won't snitch."

Shanta was protecting me while trying to use me. I didn't understand what was going on.

The short girl with the curly hair interfered. *"Yeah, how can we know he's not going to snitch?"*

"Yeah," said the ponytail doctor.

"I'm no snitch," I replied.

"So, w*ill you help us?"* asked the gym boy. I could see he was trying to restrain himself.

Will I get myself involved in a dangerous, juvenile fight against a radical militant group after I just came back from being a dead soldier? The answer was simple.

"No," I replied.

The gym boy took Shanta to the far corner of the room and spoke to her in private, and I couldn't hear anything of meaning. Then Shanta and the gym boy turned back to me. She was smiling, and looked more relaxed.

"Roy, I want you to meet the resistance. This is Bahomi," she said, pointing to the gym boy.

Stupid name for a stupid kid, I thought.

"The curly one is Toya, and next to her is Dev." She paused for a moment. "Why don't we sit down? Can we all sit?"

She was trying to be the good cop now, while this Bahomi guy was being the nasty asshole cop. We all sat down in a sort of a circle. I indeed felt the tension decrease a little. She continued.

"What we do here is not a suicide mission. We don't want to provoke a war. We are trying to educate the people about the real danger. Every day we're inside this death trap city, dependent on the systems to protect us, is another day the Purists are training and learning more about us. They have taken those years to study us, waiting for a mistake or a system failure that will allow them in. And in the meanwhile what have we done? Became numb inside a simulation of pleasure. People can't do anything for themselves rather than wait for a technician to fix the problem. They say the simulation creates stuff from your memories and subconscious, but it's always testing you in some way, so they can study you to better control you. People don't know how dangerous this way of life is, and how fragile it is. They don't know how to defend themselves against threats like the Purists, who want to steal the food and water. They assume that the resources will always be there, thanks to the mind-numbing simulations. The city needs to become human again. That's why we need you to help us train them. We're not asking you to fight; we're asking you to help us save our families."

My days of being a soldier are over. I already died once and had a new life to build. I took a deep breath.

"I'm sorry. I can't do that. Let me out."

I stood up and turned for the exit. I couldn't get involved in this farce. All I could see was a group of hormone-washed, bored teenagers who want to 'fight the system.' I could lose everything I'd gained in the past days, which wasn't much. No thanks. I count on my laser guns to save us.

Bahomi stood against the door and was blocking my way.

"*You're not going anywhere, soldier.*"

I hated him for always speaking quickly to me.

Dev, the ponytail guy and Toya held my arms behind my back. It was four against one. No one was willing to let me go, and they were losing their patience. I was getting frustrated.

"*You were a soldier, right?*" asked Bahomi, right in my face.

I didn't answer. I had had enough of this.

He got closer to my face, shouting at me. Dev and Toya grabbed me harder, holding my shoulder and keeping my arms behind my back.

"*Were you a soldier?*"

"Yes!"

"*Can you shoot a gun In the real world?*"

"Yes."

"*Can you teach others?*"

"Maybe."

Maybe he was trying to convince me that I was capable of helping them by saying yes all the time. Like I was supposed to serve and protect by the flip of a switch.

"I already died once and I'm not going to—"

"—*Isn't that a miracle? Listen to me now because soon there won't be any of us alive in here.*"

"And if you're wrong, what happens to you?" Shanta got back into the conversation.

"My mom is the president. Trust me when I tell you that the threat is real."

"So why isn't she doing anything?"

"As always, she and the council think technology will prevail, which is why they want us to stay plugged into their digital utopia. Those are the foundations of this place."

"Then why is she wrong?"

"Because we can't do it forever," said Dev directly into my ear.

Shanta stepped near me. "One day our machines will stop working and there will be no guns left and no sentinels to protect us. Hell, maybe just the air conditioning will stop working. Or there will be a bug in the program and people will have to surface."

"This place is run by quantum computers, isn't it?"

The curly-haired Toya interrupted.

"What if the whole city becomes a shooting range? Think of it. Ten thousand people, who haven't ever seen daylight because they were born into the simulation, will be held as hostages. They'd be sitting ducks."

"They will be ten thousand strong. That's power."

"If they are trained and collaborating, which they are not," Toya answered.

"How old are you?"

"Sixteen," she answered.

"And you?" I asked Bahomi.

"Same," he replied.

"This is classic."

I was exhausted of the whole debate.

"*Classic what?*" Bahomi asked with a sneer.

"Never mind."

Bahomi turned to Shanta. He looked furious and she looked disappointed.

"That's it. I'm sorry, but I told you, he's not one of us. He doesn't care."

"I am one of—"

"—*Shut up!*"

I looked at Shanta, and the cheerful Shanta whom I held on top of a whale, was gone. Who was standing there was a different person completely.

"Look, just let me go and I'll never tell anyone, ok?"

Shanta was silent and it made me angrier.

"I prefer asking nicely."

She looked at me with fire in her eyes.

Dev and Toya pushed me back and pinned me to the wall, I twisted Toya's arm and threw her at Dev but Bahomi grabbed my head and slammed it to the wall. I fell on the floor and they left before I was able to stand up.

Chapter 10

I banged on the door for awhile but no one came for me. Not even Shanta. I couldn't believe it; I was locked up by a bunch of stupid kids playing war games. I was supposed to go back to training, do my part and blend in. Now I was involved with the second most hated group in the city. And to think; Padma didn't know that her own daughter ran the show. How genius was that? I was stuck there with no food, no water and no bed. I was afraid it would take a day until Isaac or Viti sent someone to look for me, and maybe another day until somebody would find me.

My attempts to open the door were futile because it was a sliding door and I couldn't get a grip. I managed to bust open the vent for the air supply on the ceiling with my fist, but it was too high and too narrow for me to go through. I decided to rest and wait, to save my strength in case one of the resistance members came back. I sat down and dozed off.

I awoke after about an hour. A metal clunk echoed through the room and I thought someone was outside the door. The room became fully dark except for a little emergency light, which indicated there had been another power outage. Maybe the Purists attacked again. I called for help but still no one heard me. I thought about Isaac's mantra: *"Everything I said or did is my sole responsibility. Everything is connected. Everything changes."* It didn't help. I was still helpless and I started to blame myself for falling for Shanta. What a manipulative bitch.

I fell asleep again and woke up to the sudden sound of Bahomi opening the door. Why him? He touched my shoulder with painful precision to make sure I was awake.

"I'm awake, damn it."

"Come with me," he said slowly for the first time.

I got up and walked behind him, as if I had a choice.

"If this is some kind of initiation I'm not falling for it."

"Shut up."

I didn't like him and he didn't like me either. Not enough to be polite. We went through the water system corridors. They were gray and leaking. I assumed the pipes led from the sea, pumping salty water into the desalination systems. When we reached a ladder leading to a hatch above, he handed me a Cactus suit. Not again…I was still riddled with red dots. We both dressed up, though, and he did it so fast it seemed he didn't mind getting stung by the suit.

We went to the surface and the humid air stood still. There was no dust flying around and the temperature was reasonably warm. I could see the night sky so clearly. Billions of stars were looking down at us. The wind turbines were moving slowly and the cameras were scanning the grounds. The ground was dry and every step of ours sounded like we were crushing bones. The moon was half-full and low in the sky so we barely cast any shadow. He had chosen a perfect time to be out: we were like ghosts. Walking didn't hurt as much because I managed to find the right angle to spread my arms and legs. I felt stupid and I probably looked stupid but it worked just as Viti said. Crossing the circle of guns through a hole in the fence was the scary part. I knew they couldn't see me, but going out of the safe zone was ball-shrinking. And I wasn't 100% sure if my former stealth abilities could be applied while wearing a Cactus.

I followed him for a few minutes until we reached the peak of a nearby hill.

"I'm going to show you something I think is better for you to see with your own cocky eyes."

"I don't have cocky eyes."

"Yes you do. You think you are better than everyone because you died once and you are the only one who can figure shit out."

"Whatever you say."

"You think that just because you don't belong here you shouldn't be involved, but you need to see it. Because this will make you understand."

"Just show me already."

We climbed over another boulder and the air was so humid my lungs almost refused to let in the air. Bahomi crouched and then crawled to a viewpoint. I did the same but a lot slower. In the desert every sound you make carries for miles; like whale songs in the ocean.

"You find it hard to believe the city endures so many attacks and invasion attempts. You think we exaggerate."

He handed me thermal binoculars and I hung them on my neck. I watched the foot of the hill and began to see little dots of light moving around in the distance. They looked like flickering candles. I followed the light deeper into the valley and there it was, a whole city, alive and moving in the middle of the desert. There were tents and sheets of cloth stretched between them, supporting tin plates and barrels and solar panels. I could see people moving underneath the whole structure like blood cells under a skin. They were skinny, there were a lot of them, and they all carried guns.

"Do you understand what you see?"

"The Purists?"

"They have little resources. They use seismic equipment to find water, and special greenhouses to grow plants. When they can't, they destroy another group and take their resources. They just move to another place when they need to."

"They didn't destroy us yet."

"Strategic investment. They know we're worth the wait."

"Because we're self-sustained?"

"Right."

"How can they claim to be pure if they want to rely on our technology?"

"When it comes to food and water, there are no rules to these guys. They will destroy everything. Trust me, no one is pure."

I couldn't trust him even if he'd told me the earth was round.

"But they are supposed to be pure, right?"

"It's different here. We started hearing about them long ago. When the droughts began people fled north to the Arctic Circle and the Scandinavian countries, where it was still green. That's where they first hit. They even prevented scientists from developing cold fusion energy. They grew and grew and destroyed everything they came across. They were too weak to bother us at first but now they are ready. They are here and are waiting for the right opportunity."

"People join them?"

"You don't believe what people do for guaranteed food and water."

"But how do they live like that?"

"To keep themselves cool during the day they hide in underground holes. Sound familiar? They're mainly active at night, digging to find underground water reservoirs. And as for food, they grow what they can and steal what they can't. And of course share everything with their group."

"There is still water underground?"

"Imagine this ruthless heat to the other extreme during a short, monstrous winter. The rain eventually accumulates underground."

Again I was silent.

"They would love to camp outside our city and use our water and food resources. But they need to get rid of us first."

"How do you know all this?"

"I used to learn everything I could about them because I knew they would come for us one day. You have to be stupid to think they won't. Then I started watching them on the outside, counting the number of attacks and their open threats."

I was still confused. Bahomi sensed that.

"We can't beat them unless we wake everyone up before they attack us."

"They don't look like a real army, like a real threat."

"We have an informant on the security team. He keeps us up to date with reports of more invasion attempts and shots fired at the sentinels. We might be able to stop the first wave of attacks, but after that they'll destroy our defense systems, and then there will be no one to protect us."

"But what if we offered to help them?"

"The northern city offered them help a long time ago. It didn't end well."

"So we are just going to kill them all?"

"Just the ones that come for us. Then the rest will run away. For good."

"And if they come back?"

"If they come back for a second try, there won't be a third."

"It doesn't make sense. Why would Padma be so blind to this?

"She isn't. She thinks she's protecting everyone by acting natural. She thinks we can withstand the risk."

"And you are willing to risk it all?"

"We've fought them year after year. But they're small fights, like a mosquito that comes back every night and sucks more blood out of you. I've had enough of it."

He paused for a moment, appearing to wonder if he should continue. I wasn't convinced it was genuine. To me, he sounded dangerous. Just because he had enough didn't mean he should get others involved.

"Do you know what frightened me the most?" he asked, pausing again. "It's not the slaughter, the bloodshed, or the cruelty. Those things are no surprise to me because we're animals and we fight to kill, sometimes winning and sometimes losing. What frightens me is the indifference. People just don't care. They don't believe that evil exists anymore because they don't see it in their little virtual fantasies. Just like you."

Then I saw a twinkle on the other side of the slope, a tiny, white flash. I tried to listen if there was anyone there because nothing twinkles in the desert for no reason. I started to sweat down my back. Maybe they had seen our binoculars flashing.

We climbed back up the hill and headed back. The gravel made cracking sounds. If there was indeed someone close enough, they'd know where we were, so we began to walk faster to reach the top. Once we got over the ridge we'd be safe because no one without a Cactus could escape the guns and the sentinels.

A moment before we reached the top I heard footsteps behind me. I didn't see anything at first, but after a moment I saw a metal body coming right at Bahomi. It was another man in a Cactus suit. My stomach shrank, my knees bent, and my eyes opened wide. We ran like hell. It was a sprint to get to the safe zone and into the city. But if that man had a bona fide suit we were doomed.

Everything happened in less than a second. I continued running until I heard Bahomi scream. I looked back and saw the intruder knocking Bahomi's head on the ground, ignoring me completely. I took advantage of this and ran back to him, knocking him off an unconscious Bahomi as he looked around for something. The man recovered and then lunged toward me, pushing me. I rolled downhill until I got stuck on a rock. I was a couple

of feet from Bahomi. I think I heard a cracking
sound in my ribs. Then came the man in the Cactus
and started to pull the Cactus off me. He pulled hard
but a beam of light started to light our surroundings.
It was a sentinel approaching. He stopped and
leaned close to me, holding me so I couldn't move.
I could hear him gasping; his breath stank. The
sentinel shut its light and continued the patrol. I
used that split second to knee him and then throw
him away from me. I kicked him again and he lost
his balance and rolled down the hill. I stood up and
ran after him until he stopped. The sentinel came
back and scanned the hill. It started to approach us
and I crouched and breathed through my nose to
make the least possible noise I could make. Then I
picked a stone and threw it away from us to divert
the sentinel's attention. The intruder managed to
catch his breath and regain focus but he didn't
move. I approached the man slowly while gripping
the binoculars' strap. I started swinging it like a
slingshot. I got closer. He was lying on his belly
with his head toward me. He was looking at me the
whole time, and I could see the glare in his eyes
through the Cactus fibers. Then he leaned on his

side and sent his hand to his belt beneath the Cactus suit. I sprung and swung my binoculars directly to his hand. A metal clunk echoed through the desert. The pistol that he was drawing fell to the ground. I immediately jumped over and took it. I cocked it and pointed it at his head.

"Stop," I said quietly.

My mouth was dry from heaving. If I shot him the sentinel would've detected the sound and hunted me down. The intruder looked around him. I guessed he was trying to figure out what to do. I hoped the gun wasn't locked but I couldn't tell without diverting my eyes.

"Remove your Cactus," I said.

He did nothing.

"Your camouflage suit."

He continued to look at me silently.

"Undress or I'll blow your head off."

I tried to be as serious as I could without shouting or using large movements, but I didn't really know what to do. The intruder started removing all the Cactus parts. First the head, then the sleeves, and finally the shirt and pants. He looked thin and pale. His clothes were dirty with yellow desert dust and I guessed he was only a couple of years older than me by the thin beard he had.

"Sit on the ground," I commanded.

He sat, and I stood in front of him to block the sentinel's camera and scanners.

"Where did you get this suit from?"

"We make our own."

I thought he would've had an Arabic accent, but he had a normal Israeli accent. My perception of the Purists was wrong already.

"Did you spy on us?"

"Did *you* spy on *us*?"

"Are you planning an attack?"

He started laughing a dry, flat laugh that sounded degrading. I got angrier. This is not the way to play when someone is pointing a gun to your head.

"Are *you* planning an attack?" he replied with a smirk.

"Don't play with me," I said.

"Or what? You are going to shoot me?"

"I'll let the sentinel chase you around first. That'll be less pleasant."

He stopped smiling.

"When is the attack?" I asked.

"Why do you think I will tell you, stupid boy?"

"Because if you want to return home, you will tell me."

"You kill me and they change the day. I return and they change the day anyway."

"But you can prevent other people's deaths."

"It's not on me, or you. The decision has been made a long time ago. With me or without me, it doesn't make any difference."

"You can never breach this place. Your leaders are sending people to their deaths."

"Oh boy, they didn't teach you anything inside. We've already won."

"We can kill you all and stop it."

"Yeah? So why haven't you? You are stuck in your bunker, passive and numb. We grow in numbers, train, build weapons. We will terminate you like stepping on an ants' nest."

A sound of a roaming sentinel approached. I got up and pointed the gun to the ground.

"Tell them they shouldn't try to do it."

"Are you releasing me?"

"Yes."

"Why?"

"Like you said. It won't change anything."

He laughed again. I wanted to put a bullet in his head just to make him stop laughing at me all the time, but I couldn't let myself.

"Go!"

"You could've killed me, but the inside made you weak."

"Go!"

"Remember this boy, as long as people are addicted to technology and power, they will continue to destroy the world. Look around, we've already won."

I aimed the gun at him and pointed at the hill. I could have killed him, but I don't shoot prisoners. That's what I'd been taught, and it was still in me. Shanta would think I agreed to help them, but I couldn't take sides or bring him in alive for questioning.

I had to go back unnoticed, so I followed him with the pistol while he ran up the hill. He walked slowly and then stopped, and then turned around and shot me. He had another gun all along. I fired at his direction instinctively. The sentinel heard that for sure. I dropped to the ground. A moment after, I saw a flash of light behind me and then his body rolling down the hill until he lay still on the ground. The sentinel would be back for me. I couldn't do anything, and lay there for I don't know how long. I tried to stay conscious, letting the pain rush through me. I couldn't fight it, anyway.

The stars were looking at me; just a grain of dust. Shadows passed before my eyes, although I wasn't blacking out. It was Bahomi reaching to get me. I allowed myself to pass out.

Chapter 11

I woke up in a jail cell. I had bandages on my stomach, and it felt like somebody had put broken glass in there and sewn me back up. Other than that, everything was intact. I finally remembered what had happened when the anesthetic wore off. *How could I let the intruder go? Why didn't I frisk him? How did I let him shoot me? Have I forgotten everything they taught me in the army?* I felt so stupid.

Regarding the cell situation, first I was scared but then I realized it at least meant I was alive and not assimilated. At least not yet. I didn't know what was coming to me. After all, I did disobey Padma.

After calming down I had a more relevant thought: the invasion was real. The Purists would eventually come for us. The resistance was right and I blew them off.

I analyzed my every mistake, every miscalculation. I didn't take a gun, and I didn't cover the lens to avoid reflections. I got too far down the hill. I passed the gun circle. And how come no one is doing anything but the resistance?

And why did I let Bahomi take me there in the first place?

Dr. Ashish came to examine me and the cell door buzzed open. He lifted the blanket and the bandage.

"The laser stitching looks good. No infection, just swelling."

Then he pulled out a little sonogram device that looked like an old telephone—but way cooler—and pointed it at my wound.

"Tissues are already reconnecting. I think you'll survive this one."

"Thanks. For everything."

"Just doing my job."

"Do you know what's going to happen with me?"

"You will live."

"No, I mean this." I pointed at the cell bars, yet he remained silent.

"It's not good, Roy."

He seemed worried and I wanted to change the subject.

"Have you found anything about my parents?"

"I have good news and bad news."

"Give me the bad first."

"I'm afraid they go together."

"Ok." I was ready for impact.

"I asked the guys over at the northern city. They reported that your parents did get defrosted but they vanished twenty years ago."

"Twenty years ago?"

"Your parents were alive after defrosting. But no one has seen them since the Purist attack twenty years ago."

"Are you sure?"

"I'm afraid so. I don't know what happened to them, but I do know they didn't come here."

"Someone must have more details. Didn't they have security cameras?"

"They did."

"So how can I see the video from that day?"

"It's probably classified, and I don't have clearance."

President Padma buzzed herself into my cell. I tried to sit straight for her, but it hurt. She noticed.

"Stay as you are."

"President Padma," said Dr. Ashish.

I could see how removed she was. She wasn't pleased to see me. She signaled Dr. Ashish to leave us, which he did with a little head tilt. She waited until he left.

"Do you know why I invited you onstage in front of everybody?"

"So I would feel part of this city," I said with remorse.

"Yes, that's also the reason I gave you that job. So you had everything you wanted but still endangered us."

I think I was beyond the point of pulling the innocent defrosty card.

"The Purist, he said something about an invasion."

"The invasion has been happening for fifty years now. Nothing has changed. We have always been attacked. It doesn't matter. Our systems have always kept us safe."

"What happens if our systems fail?"

"It won't happen."

"How can you be sure?"

"Because I have people who fix the systems, people who care about this place, and whom I can trust."

Ouch.

"He said they already won."

She giggled as if she had heard this before.

"Humans caused the crisis and the Purists just made it worse. They are human, after all. If we can't learn anything about ourselves here, we will never change. The simulation is the only guarantee of change because it helps us identify the causes and effects of our ill nature."

They blame us, we blame them. It's a never-ending cycle.

"How long do I stay here?"

"Until the council decides what your punishment will be."

She was about to leave when I stopped her.

"I need to know what happened to my parents."

"I can't help you anymore."

"I need access to the videos of the Purist attack on the northern city twenty years ago."

"Those are classified."

"I need to know what happened, I might see something."

"You just breached our security and almost got kidnapped. What makes you think I'm going to let you have access to classified information?"

"Because you just said you care about your children. And so did my parents."

"Nice try, but you're up for assimilation or exile. There's no use searching for your parents anymore."

She left, and I was more angry and confused than before. If she was aware of the threat, how could she be so certain about the city's safety? How could she do nothing? I didn't expect her to reveal all the secret plans, but I'd been taught long ago that when someone tells you not to worry, and that everything is fine, that means everything is not just fine and you should start worrying. It wasn't even a week ago for me when prime ministers, government members and generals used me to try to calm the nation with such messages. They told us how strong and united we were, and how much we're a highly sophisticated and highly trained nation with the best soldiers and the most advanced army technology.

Guess what? I died on that assumption. And I didn't want to die on it again.

Chapter 12

That night, I awoke because I heard a loud click coming from the cell door. The cell was pitch-black, and no emergency lights were on.

"Hello?"

No one answered.

I stayed in bed for a moment. I was woozy and I didn't know if I was allowed to stand up. Not that I could see where I was walking.

"Come with us," a familiar voice whispered. It was Shanta.

The cell door hinges squeaked. I sat on my bed and reached out with my legs. A warm hand grabbed mine. My bare feet felt the stingy metal rod of the Cactus suit. I followed the silent swoosh of the Cactus in pitch-black, knowing I was being led to freedom outside. The only directions I got were in whispers: *"Left, right, faster, watch the door."* I was totally blind yet fully aware at the same time. Only when we got to the service tunnel did Bahomi turn on a dimmed red flashlight so I could put on the Cactus. We climbed outside. The moon was thin and a layer of dust shrouded the stars.

"How did you do it?" I whispered.

"We have a man on the inside," Bahomi said.

"We're *not* just a bunch of teenagers playing resistance," Shanta added.

We walked in silence, getting far from the city. After a few minutes we heard gunfire and saw the city's laser guns fire. It almost felt normal. We kept going south for about thirty minutes until we reached a large cave opening. The air was hot and humid, and I briefly imagined a cold shower that would never happen. We went inside the cave, holding bright flashlights. The cave was as big as four buses standing next to each other. In some corners you could've seen boulders that had fallen from the cave's ceiling. Bahomi pulled out two cushions and two dusty mattresses that were hidden behind one of the boulders. The air was cool and nice. We took off our Cactus suits and lay them on the ground.

"Wow," I sighed. "This is awesome."

"Better get used to it, you're going to be here for awhile," said Shanta.

"You two live out here?" I asked.

"Sometimes." They looked at each other briefly.

"And the Purists haven't found this place?"

"Not yet," she said, sitting on one of the cushions. "We don't start a fire or leave any remains when we come here."

Bahomi pulled a mattress and joined us.

"Here, we have something to show you." He was holding a square of firm yet flexible paper.

"What I'm about to show you is top secret," he said in a somewhat mechanical tone, slow and serious.

He turned to the screen and moved the slider to the beginning of the video. The first video was a high-angle shot of the city perimeter. There was a man standing in the sun next to a carriage tied to a donkey, wearing a white robe. Bahomi started to comment on the video as it played.

"At 19:00 the Purist leader was standing outside the city's main gate. The negotiation was held over AM radio transmissions during the previous weeks. He requested food for his people in return for a ceasefire." The video cut to another angle of the surroundings of the city. "Our surveillance continued to scan the area for any movement."

A video from inside the main gate showed the door rolling up and three sentinels traveling out. Two stopped just outside the door while it rolled down again. The third sentinel moved towards the man, carrying a large box.

"A month's worth of food supplies were packed in a cold container. The man spoke to the sentinel's microphone and insisted that the amount was not enough—despite having agreed upon that amount ahead of time—and that he would wait for more."

I could see the man's face through the sentinel's camera. He was young and slim. If you would only look at his eyes you would say he was in his thirties, yet the deep wrinkles next to his eyes and mouth made him look like he was fifty. He looked like life was a burden to him, but a burden that he was willing to take on and on.

The video was moving in fast-forward yet continued to play.

"After an hour of debating, the man was still standing there silent and motionless. It was about

120 degrees Fahrenheit and 96% humidity. Yet he didn't move an inch. The city council had decided to send another sentinel with more food. Two sentinels were still guarding the front, and a fourth sentinel was sent out to the Purist leader to carry out the extra box. The two boxes were placed on a carriage tied to the donkey, and then the Purist leader started to walk the donkey away from the city perimeter."

"Why did they do it?" I wasn't naive; I knew something was about to happen.

"The northern city had disobeyed Padma. She told them not to negotiate with the Purists to begin with."

The video continued.

"By the time the Purist leader had reached the nearby hills, eight rockets were fired from outside the city in the sentinels' direction. And the main door hadn't fully rolled up yet. At this stage, New Knaan received the emergency signal. They deployed combat drones as backup for the northern city, knowing that they might take up to twenty minutes to fly across sixty-five miles."

I could see the explosions from the camera inside the gate. The main door was immediately shut.

"One sentinel was hit but remained functional. Three other sentinels were directed to shoot at the source of the rockets. The cameras detected multiple movements along the surrounding hills and fired there as well. The guns were shooting almost at 180 degrees east of the city. More rockets were fired from multiple directions, demobilizing one sentinel, although it retained the ability to fire back."

The video showed three sentinels scattering and firing at targets off the screen.

"Two hundred yards from the main gate, twenty Purists exited underground tunnels and destroyed the three remaining sentinels."

The video showed the battlefield with four smoking sentinels and laser guns exploding one by one. The twenty Purists were moving toward the inner circle of the guns.

"The Purists were wearing camouflage gear similar to ours and were hard to detect, so we switched to intruder override and began to shoot any suspicious movement inside the safe zone. One of them managed to blow out one of our emergency hatches and went inside. Five Purists followed him. That was the point where our drones arrived and started to attack from the air."

The screen displayed four camera views of four drones launching missiles at groups of Purists who emerged from the surrounding hills. By now they were attacking the city by the hundreds. No matter who got hit, others continued toward the city.

"What happened inside?" I asked.

"These videos are too classified, we couldn't get them," Shanta said.

"The Purists kept pouring in, most of them wearing camouflage. Since it was dusk, they cast no shadow. Their leader's stalling had been precious to them because when the city council was debating over ratios, daylight had been running out. The drones showed northern citizens running out of the emergency hatches, looking thin and weak. They ran and fell, got up and stumbled again. That's when the Purists got to the citizens. Some were shot dead on the spot. Some were taken into the attack tunnels the Purists had dug in front of the city. Then laser guns even fired at citizens who were about to get abducted. The drones then started to shoot the opening of the tunnels so they would collapse."

Shanta was wrong: the people weren't numb, and their survival instincts were working. But they were working in the wrong way. It was flight instead of fight. Instead of hiding inside, where the citizens had a slight advantage over the Purists, the citizens ran right into the Purists' trap. They knew they had to do something, but that something got them killed.

"At that point only a quarter of the laser guns remained functional. Then Purists began to draw back. The ones that breached the city were killed. The others ran out of ammunition and pulled back. Our drones were out of missiles as well, but kept on circling the perimeter to send video feed."

When it seemed to be over, no more shots were fired. I saw *them*. They looked different. More hunched, more bent. They didn't run but walked fast, a man and a woman, holding hands. The man was holding a gun, and they both had sacks tied to their backs. They escaped west into the valley. The drones' video turned away from that direction and they went out of the frame, opposite of the Purists' location.

My parents were alive, at least back then.

Then it hit me: I thought I knew what I was doing but actually I didn't. I thought I wanted to find my parents, to save myself, to get Shanta to like me and help the resistance to save the city. But after seeing the attack I actually didn't want any of that.

Shanta wasn't happy to see me.

Bahomi hated me because he thought that I was trying to steal Shanta and ruin his operation.

And my parents were probably dead already.

I wanted to live, but this new world wasn't worth living in. I thought I wanted to belong, but besides the people who wanted to use me, I had no one to belong to. I realized none of the things I wanted mattered anymore.

No courting Shanta, no fighting Bahomi, no finding my parents and definitely no pleasing Padma. No more Roy the follower. I had to help save ten thousand Knaan people in any way possible.

"So what will it be?" said Shanta.

"Thank you for rescuing me."

"Cut the crap," said Bahomi, "and say what you want to say."

"I saved your life."

"And I saved yours."

"Could you please forget your stupid man pride for just a few minutes?" Shanta said.

"You were there just like me, you saw who they are," Bahomi said, facing me. "Are you going to help us kill those Purists or not?!" he yelled.

Shanta was looking at me impatiently. That was the million-dollar question and I already declined the first time.

"I am going to help you defend the city."

"Same thing," Bahomi interrupted.

"It's not the same thing," I insisted.

"Can you believe this prick?" Bahomi said to Shanta. "After we rescued him just now."

"Would you just let him speak? Damnit!" Her face turned red.

Bahomi kept quiet and lowered his eyes. What was going on between them before I came?

"Why isn't it the same thing?" she asked me.

"I talked to the Purist before he died. I know what our guns are capable of. And I agree that the people are numb. But scaring them into joining you isn't going to help. You saw the video: there will be chaos. Most people in danger either hide or run for their lives. They will be helpless inside if the Purists get in, and they will be helpless outside if they run away. That's why we have to train them—"

"—I told you he was going to say something like that," Bahomi interrupted again.

"Shut up, let him finish," Shanta said, owning him.

I decided to address Shanta and ignore him. I'd deal with him later.

"You told me you tried raising awareness but it didn't work. You tried to scare them and that didn't work either. Disconnecting all at once would just cause panic, and your mother would just reassure them that the guns are ok and they would all go back to sleep. Then she'd assimilate us all for treason."

"How do we know he's not working for her right now?" Bahomi asked Shanta while ignoring me back.

I looked at Shanta, who didn't stop Bahomi this time.

"How do we know she didn't brainwash him when she visited him in the clinic? How do we know that he is not disrupting our plan just so she could stop us?"

I looked at Shanta.

"I'll train you so you could train others inside. And when the Purists come we'll be ready. We will be able to fight back."

"How long will it take?" she asked.

"It depends on the people. At least six months, maybe more."

"We don't have six months. I told you he's going to push our plans back," Bahomi said quietly.

"That's the only logical way," I said.

"You think Padma is that stupid that she won't notice so much activity?" He lashed at me.

Shanta was quiet the whole time.

"I need you all to train them on the inside and command them. We need at least a hundred people, if not more—"

"—Every day we don't disconnect the people is suicide," Bahomi said to Shanta.

Shanta looked at him, but didn't know what to say anymore.

"We can't gamble on six more months. And what if Padma assimilates us all? Don't you think it will look suspicious?" he asked.

"Not if you do it in small groups."

"That takes even more time!"

"I'm just trying to answer your question." I was already boiled up.

"If we disconnect everybody she won't be able to stop us anyway."

"But I am trying to tell you that—"

"—It's bullshit!" he shouted and got too close to me. He was trying to be the alpha but I couldn't let him.

"Shut up both of you. I can't think!" Shanta said.

"Let me ask you something, Bahomi. Do you exercise a lot?"

"Yes."

"Do you think you could fight them?"

"Damn right."

"Why?"

"Because I trained myself."

"Show me."

"Show you what?"

I lunged towards Bahomi with a right hook. He took the hit and came back at me with a left hook to the ribs. I blocked his punch and pushed him away so I could kick his stomach. He toppled down on his knees.

"Painful, right? Can't you fight with real pain? Oh yeah, you never actually experienced real pain in your simulation training."

He got up and tried to kick and punch me a couple of times. I avoided his hits or blocked them. Every time I evaded I gave him a punch to the stomach until he could go no more.

He fell to his knees again, gasping. Shanta stood next to him and touched his shoulder. He waved her hand away.

"That's why you need to train for six months outside of the simulation. You think you're quick because it's in your mind. But your body isn't ready until you train it physically."

Shanta looked even more confused. I turned to her.

"Same goes for gun training, by the way."

"What if your idea fails?" she asked. "What if we can't prepare them on time? What if no one joins your fun activity?"

"What happens if *your* plan *succeeds*?" I replied. "Let's say we block the invasion. Then what? You think all the people wouldn't want to escape back **into** the simulation? The remaining Purists would still be outside waiting for their next opportunity."

Again I was met with their silence and their wondering faces, which revealed everything to me.

"You didn't even wonder what would happen if you were successful, did you?"

Bahomi raised his eyes at me.

"That won't happen because they will not survive. It's either we kill them all or they run away someplace else."

"And what do you think?" I asked Shanta.

"I don't think we need to stay here at all," she said.

"So where would we go?"

"North, as north as we can; where we can still live outside."

"And do you even know what's out there?"

"We need to get there and join the rest of the free people. This place won't hold us for much longer; the power grid is weak and we're under constant attack. Put it together."

"Who will accept ten thousand people? You don't know what goes on there and who's fighting whom. How many resources are there to share with others?"

"It doesn't matter now. First we need to win this or else we have no future anyway," said Shanta.

"That sounds a lot like the Purists, doesn't it? Moving from place to place, consuming and exhausting resources," I said.

"There are abandoned facilities, research labs, schools and hospitals we can use. My mom has friends that can help us get settled there. It's been offered before."

"You have no idea what you're going for and what are the consequences," I stressed. "You have this desire to destroy everything but no plan for a new order that you want to create."

Shanta was devastated. I didn't want to attack her like that but she had to understand that I was most qualified to lead this thing.

"Fine, we'll go with your plan for now," she said. I could see the wetness in her eyes.

Bahomi got on his feet and stormed out of the cave.

"We start tomorrow. I'll gather the others."

I could tell she wanted to go after him, but I stopped her.

"How many guns do we have?"

"There's enough for a thousand years."

"What about ammunition?"

"When they built this place they entered the entire world's crisis data into a quantum computer. It gave predictions of how many incidents the city should expect. We have supplies for even worse than the worst prediction. The only part not ready is the people."

That's another thing that fed Padma's false belief that the city could survive on technology alone.

"And how do we mask our activity inside the simulation? I don't want them to suspect there's something going on," I said.

"Don't worry. We have a guy on the inside."

"And he is…?"

"He masks our digital activities and wipes security camera footage for us. That's why we can all meet here with no one tracing us."

"Who is this guy?"

"Let's just say he believes in our cause. We're not just a bunch of kids playing war like you said."

She faced the door, hesitated, and then turned back to me.

"Thank you for helping us. I know it was difficult for you to make this decision."

Chapter 13

For a month we were all cramped inside the cave that turned super-hot after all the physical exercises. But hey, it was super-hot outside as well and we had to prepare for the worst. I gave close-combat Krav Maga lessons. Personally, I hated that fighting system because it was too aggressive and lacked the beauty of Eastern martial arts. It resembled the Israeli attitude: graceless, without manners, cut to the point with no style. But it was designed to neutralize an enemy in the fastest way possible and we had no time to dive deep in Eastern fighting philosophies.

My job was to make sure that our weaknesses would be lying beneath many layers of muscle and skill. If you want to be brave and fight in a closed, narrow space, you have to trust your body and skills, not guns. Shanta, Bahomi, Toya and Dev's posture were better, and I could see their muscles were bigger. Their gaze was more focused and calm, like snipers waiting for the target to appear. We ate so much bug-goo to maintain our growing muscles, yet it wasn't enough, and I didn't feel as strong as I used to back in my real Army training. Luckily, the inside guy had masked the surge in food production data and smuggled bug-goo packs for breakfast, lunch and dinner.

They hadn't lain in simulation beds all day long, which was another part they had to mask. So they created their own avatars to play around in the simulation in case someone was looking for them. While the others sneaked in and out to the city, I stayed in the cave. I had one working gun with ammunition with me in case any Purist discovered the cave. I wondered how the Purists didn't smell me after so many days of sweating and without taking a decent shower.

On the last day of the first month Bahomi caught up with me after we finished our session.

"If something happens to Shanta, I'll kill you," he said.

"I'm not stealing her from you."

I was honest. That girl wasn't stable; she tricked me into liking her so she could take advantage of my skills. She lied and manipulated me to become a soldier again. Not the ideal date, I would say. She was attractive, she was smart, but deep down I was still hurt.

He repeated his threat and then he walked back toward the city.

That night, I decided to go back inside to take a damn shower. It'd been a month already and, although I got used to the smell and dirt, I felt like I deserved a treat. Shanta arranged for the security camera footage to be erased, but I still I had to keep a low profile, and do it quickly.

I went back to the gym late to use the shower. It was empty. When I got out, though, Isaac was there sitting on a bench and stretching. He was shocked to see me, and then he became angry. I felt like a teenager being caught doing something bad.

"Where have you been?" he asked.

"Away."

"Away where?"

I could say nothing to him, and didn't have time to make up an explanation either. So I just started walking. But he blocked my way: angry, old, and looking right at me.

"I can't tell you."

"You're supposed to be in jail, everyone's been looking for you."

"President's punishment."

"Don't lie to me. I tell stories; I can smell a lie from miles away."

"What do you want?" I said while trying to leave again.

He blocked my way. Something was different about him; he was frightening.

"Don't think me for a fool. Wounded in a fight with a Purist, and then escaping jail. Everything's just too obvious."

"That what?"

"You're part of the resistance."

My heart stopped. I felt every vein shrink in my body. I kept a frozen face.

"No I'm not," I said in a soft tone, "I'm just trying to survive."

He looked at me like he didn't believe me. And why shouldn't he? He read me like a billboard. I tried to divert and smiled.

"I was hiding until I could figure out what to do."

That was the truth, but only part of it.

"Listen to me, my wife is in this simulation. She's having the best time ever. She's happy and unaware of everything that's happening outside. I'm the only one who can keep her safe, ok?"

"Ok…"

"So I won't let anything happen to her. I don't know what your plan is, but if I feel that even something as minor as a cockroach's fart is about to happen—I'll tell Padma all about you and your resistance game."

"I'm not a part of a resistance, why won't you believe me?"

I could hear Bahomi shouting in my head 'Just kill him!' I was indeed close enough to break his neck but I couldn't do that and I couldn't have him expose us either. He didn't realize that he and his wife are in greater danger than he thought. But if he did tell Padma, that'd be the end of me.

"So tell me the truth, what do you do?" he asked again, as if to give me another chance. He apparently didn't want to turn to extremes, either.

"I'm just…"

"If you try to lie to me one more time I swear on my soul I'll tell Padma."

"Ok, I'll tell you, I swear, but please don't tell Padma." I played innocent.

"Let's hear it."

"Do you think THEY can hear us here?" I said softly, pointing toward the ceiling.

"Who?"

"I don't know; anyone who might be listening. Do they plant microphones in here?"

I didn't want anyone to listen to our conversation more than they had to.

He moved back and pointed toward the showers. We both squeezed inside and he turned the shower on. We stood near it fully clothed, our voices shrouded by the sound of the shower cycle.

I spoke quietly.

"I go out of the gun circle. I go on walks alone, I run and exercise."

He looked shocked, like he had trouble believing me.

"That's what you do?"

"I go in and out alone all the time."

"How do you do that?"

"There's a secret way, through an old service tunnel. Isaac, I just have to be outside. I can't stay inside this gray prison 24/7."

"I see," he said, looking calm. He apparently believed me, but looked like he didn't know what to do with what I just said to him.

"What if another Purist attacks you? What if you get kidnapped?" he asked, apparently fearing for me.

"Then it's *my* problem. The guns keep you and your wife safe like they always do."

He didn't know what to think. My story fitted my extreme circumstances exactly.

"I can take you outside; you told me that you've never been out there," I said.

"I haven't."

"You can't tell anyone."

"I won't," he said.

I was exhausted. A couple of minutes after, I took him outside. We followed the same tunnel Bahomi had shown me before, wearing Cactus suits. It looked like he was so happy, both to be going outside and to be wearing that damned suit for the first and last time. I was like his father now, taking him by the hand and showing him something spectacular he'd remember forever.

We came closer to the hatch.

"You can't be out there for long."

"It's ok, I just want to see."

Before I opened the hatch I put a piece of metal under the hatch's sensor so it would read the hatch as closed, like Bahomi taught me. Then I pulled myself out and reached inside to help Isaac out. I closed the hatch and we sat on the ground watching the night sky. If you were ever in the desert you probably knew what we saw. We could see the Milky Way, stars scattered like sugar grains in blueberry pudding. I don't know why that metaphor came to my mind but I could actually see myself taking a spoonful of that sky. Isaac took a long breath.

"I used to look at the sky from a whole different planet," I said. "What happened to this place?" It was more of a general wonder than an actual question but Isaac apparently also felt philosophical because he started storytelling again.

"You can't control everything all the time. Ever since the dawn of humanity we've tried controlling everything out of fear. We've feared the dark, fire, rain, hunger, growing old and dying. So in order to control X we invented Y. But Y always created another fear. We feared nature so we invented gods. When the gods didn't bring rain we feared hunger so we invented agriculture. We feared wild animals so we invented weapons. But then people started using weapons against each other. So we began to fear each other so we invented rules and governments to keep people safe and deal with the criminals. We feared immorality so we invented laws but then others began to punish by their own laws. We feared death so we invented medicine and medical procedures. Then we feared gene manipulation. We invented computers to control information and then we feared robots would take our jobs or kill us."

That was a lot to take in.

"Whenever we tried to control something we only made it worse by creating a new problem, along with the opportunity to carry it out. We made more complex and sophisticated systems that became too hard to control. We created industries that ruined our planet. We watched it get destroyed through our expensive lenses and screens because we needed more products and energy to control our life. So we had to go underground, because there was nothing left to control outside. There was no other way to control civil war and starvation. So our only solution was to control ourselves in simulations. We became digital gods. This world is not the best place to live in but we have no other place to go. That's the only thing we have left."

"There's not much difference between us and the Purists," I said. "We stay underground using green technologies to sustain ourselves until the atmosphere settles, and they want to destroy all corrupt technologies so the world will settle."

"We're all human; we all need to wait until the world will be habitable again. The difference is that we take care of ourselves without causing more harm, while they are exploiting and destroying everything for their own interest."

I didn't say anything for a long moment. I had to let everything he said sink in.

"I understand your fear for your wife, but if you say we can't control anything over time, then why even bother?"

"Because I love her." He then stared into my eyes.

"We do irrational things for the ones we love, even if we know it's futile."

He gazed at the sky.

I had nothing else to add. I just lied to the first friend I made here, and hoped he believed me. I didn't know what would happen to him during an invasion, or what would happen to his wife. I could just offer him a peaceful experience right now in hopes that any thought he had about reporting me was subdued by the sky.

We sat there for a couple more minutes breathing in the sky. He cried.

"I'm going back inside," he told me. "Thank you for this."

"It's the least I can do."

Once he got back, I closed the hatch from the outside and walked all the way to the cave, making sure no one was following me. After I reached the cave I pulled out a mattress and lay on my back with my eyes closed, as if I was about to enter the simulation. I just needed to rest from having the responsibility of all the constant planning.

I closed my eyes and imagined the last day with my friends on the beach. It felt weird just imagining without the simulation's aid: it felt lacking. In my own imagination, Noam and Dan were sitting next to me drinking their beers, staring at the waves. Everything was quiet: no war, no armies, and no worries. I looked at them and they seemed so peaceful and relaxed. Their expression was projected by my mind's desire onto their figures. Now I needed my own lightness, even if it was superficial and banal. I wanted Hadar. I started to miss her again so I imagined her sitting next to me, smoking, which I hated, so I made it go away. She was looking at the waves, waiting for me to create her first words. She had mocha skin and green eyes, silky black hair and a nose piercing. Back in my old life I hated when she took long, silent moments because I wanted to know what was going on inside her head. I slid my finger on her shoulder. She smiled. I remember her skin was smooth as a peach's. I lay down and put my head on her thigh. She leaned over and kissed me with her full lips. You might suspect I was horny but I wasn't. I just wanted a place to rest inside my mind inside the dark cave. Only then I could finally realize why Knaan's simulation was built: so one could escape Knaan from time to time.

Being locked inside a shelter could be damned depressing, even if it was built to save your life. But it could be just as depressing to be 'free' in a ruined outside world.

Chapter 14

I felt confident with my plan. Knaan had to be saved to save not only the active citizens' lives, but also those within the simulation. We couldn't disconnect them from their comfort just because we felt it was the right thing to do. Their fantasy was real to them, it was their entire life. And as Isaac chose reality over assimilating with his wife, they will need to do the same out of free will.

The second month of training had begun. We were all tired. Our bodies hadn't yet adapted to the change in lifestyle because our nutrition was not sufficient. Despite this, our reflexes and stamina became better.

Shanta walked inside the cave holding the flexible screen. Bahomi, Dev, Toya and I were waiting for her. We gathered around her.

"This is a conversation my mom had last night with Monish, the captain of the floating city."

"What floating city?" I asked.

"It's a ship as big as two aircraft carriers. It houses the world's richest people. They moved there in the beginning of the climate crisis and they are helping people all over the world."

She played the video on the paper screen and President Padma appeared as people usually did in a video conference.

"Monish, long time no see."

"Always a pleasure, dear Padma."

Monish looked like an aged movie star. He was a blue-eyed man in his late-forties, but you could see he had some work done on himself.

"What are you doing in this part of the world?" asked Padma.

"Actually, I'm afraid I have some bad news for you. We are sailing north from South Africa and just got these satellite images."

The flexible screen showed a bird's-eye view of a building caught on fire and military tanks standing next to it.

"They have tanks?" Padma asked with a hint of fear.

I raised my eyes at Shanta and asked quietly, "The Purists?" She nodded.

Monish continued. "Yes, they managed to find two more after all these years. Do you know where this is taken?"

"I have no idea," said Padma.

"It's the research lab near Vinnufossen."

President Padma looked shock and paused for a moment.

I looked up at Shanta again. She whispered, "Norway".

"So I guess there's nothing we can do for them?" said Padma.

"I'm afraid not."

"It's a horrible loss."

"I know," added Monish. "I just wanted to show you this as a warning. Things are heating up in the north. We don't know how those savages will surprise us."

"I know, thank you for your showing me this."

"Keep your eyes open and your teams alert. They tend to raise activities in other areas as an inspiration from one victory."

"Of course, my dear."

"I have to go. It's always a pleasure talking to you. I hope we can have more time to chat once we reach the Mediterranean."

"All the best, send my regards to your men and to Jonas."

"I will." Monish signed off.

Shanta rolled the screen into a scroll. There was an intense silence in the cave. We were all looking at each other's reactions.

I've cut the silence. "This doesn't change our plans."

"This changes everything," said Bahomi.

"It doesn't matter how they attack us. What matters is whether or not we're ready," I added.

"No, it means that we have to strike fast, before they manage to collect more weapons."

We were all looking at Shanta for a verdict.

"This doesn't change our plans."

I felt relief.

"But even Monish warned your mom," Bahomi said angrily. "They're not stupid!"

"End of discussion," Shanta said with a tone that resembled her mother's.

"But I—"

"—We came here to train. Our plan is final."

I could now see how Shanta and Bahomi had gradually grown apart. They used to stand next to each other and spar together. Now they barely made eye contact. I felt sorry for them, but it was their fault for asking me in.

When we finished warming up the training there was a shadow cast from the cave's mouth. Six guards dressed in Cactus suits stormed in holding guns. Padma walked in behind them looking like a robot version of herself: expressionless. She was dressed in a Cactus, too. Shanta and Bahomi looked at each other with terror in their eyes. I jumped aside and grabbed my gun that was leaning against a boulder. I pointed it at Padma.

"Drop it!" she shouted, fearless. "Your nonsense is over."

All that training was for nothing now that we were being held at gunpoint.

"MOM NO!" Shanta yelled.

They soldiers shot us with tranquilizer darts.

"He worked for her. He did this to us!" Bahomi shouted before dropping unconscious.

I managed to think just two quick thoughts before drowning in the blackness. Did Isaac snitch? Did Padma spy on me all along?

Chapter 15

I woke up with a terrible headache on an unfamiliar bed. Shanta was sitting next to me, stroking my hair. Her hand was so gentle.

"What happened?" I asked.

"Don't worry about it. It's all over now."

"What—"

"—I talked with my mom, I confessed everything."

"And she just let us go?"

"She finally understood what we were fighting for."

I sat on the bed feeling dizzy. I looked around and the room looked brighter for some reason. Maybe I was more sensitive to light after getting shot with a tranquilizer.

Shanta was radiating with happiness.

"I was waiting for you to wake up…you napped for so long."

She handed me a cup of water. I drank it in four big gulps.

"So, what exactly happened?"

"I broke up with Bahomi."

"Oh," I said with genuine surprise.

"'*Oh*'? Aren't you happy?"

"Well yeah."

I was too tired to show any emotion.

"I saw how you looked at me all the time."

I moved the back of my finger across her cheek. It felt incredibly smooth. That was the most I could do in that state of dizziness.

"I'm sorry it didn't work out for you two."

"It was my decision. He became unbearable."

"I know, he's a crazy fanatic."

I smiled but I bet I looked like I was missing a lobe. My face was jelly.

"I think you're still sleepy."

"I am."

"Let's get you something to eat."

I followed Shanta through the main street. We were holding hands and that was the only sensation I could focus on. Her hand felt so soft. Not like a hand of a resistance warrior. Everything felt distant, like I was riding on a cloud of tranquilizer numbness.

"Your mom, is she going to tighten up security?"

"She will."

"And we can train more people?"

"Yup."

I hadn't seen her so joyful. Something had profoundly changed. Maybe getting caught was a good thing. I had a feeling Padma wouldn't assimilate her own daughter.

"What about people staying numb inside?"

"We're still debating that. We're thinking to have a program that requires you to disconnect from the simulation a minimum of two to three hours every day to help the community. Like painting, cleaning, fixing stuff. Maybe even exercise. I don't know how people will receive it, but it's worth a shot."

"All that from one talk you never had courage to have?"

"It was an excessively long talk. Just shouting at the beginning. Some crying at the end."

"Wow."

I felt the daze start to fade away. All that risk for nothing. All they needed was to talk to each other and bring all the issues to the surface. It sounded too good to be true but it made my life much easier.

I had to pry a little more.

"And you never spoke with her about it before." My tone had a little skepticism in it, and I hoped she wasn't offended.

"Of course I did, when I was younger. But it hit a wall. I felt like she just dismissed everything I said because she alone knew what was best for the city."

"That the people are all her children and such?"

"Yeah, that bullshit. Try being the daughter of an important and smart woman telling you she doesn't want to listen to your paranoia no more. And that she has so many other children to take care of."

"I would form a resistance, I guess."

We laughed together. It felt so good to be out in the open about it. We reached the dining hall I saw on my second day in Knaan. There were people eating delicious-looking dishes. Everyone greeted her. Then we found an empty table and sat.

"What would you like?" she asked.

"What time is it?"

"It's time for breakfast. Eggs? Cheese? Salad?"

"I don't want to eat that bug-algae shit. It makes me nauseous."

"Oh no, the salad is real this time."

"Real? As in grown?"

"Yes, we have hydroponic labs that grow vegetables."

"So how come I had to eat that crap all the time?"

"Because we can't grow enough for everyone. That's just for people on duty."

"Holy shit!"

I was too loud and everyone stared at me. I lowered my voice immediately.

"Of course I want a real salad."

"Coming up."

She walked towards the vending mechanism on the other side of the room.

Everybody was minding their own business like nothing happened. But maybe it was deliberate, to keep the resistance scandal quiet. How would it look like if people found out that the president's daughter was the leader of the resistance all along? None of us had been publicly identified. It was a tranquilizer that killed our idea and some family diplomacy that revived it in a new form. I still didn't know whether it was Isaac who snitched or Padma who spied. Could it be Bahomi? Regardless, it had turned out for the best. No more hiding. No more living a double life.

Shanta came back with our dishes. I got a pretty large salad with tomatoes, cucumbers, onions, and green leaves. No dressing, though. She got herself a shakshuka, which is basically eggs poached in vegetable ratatouille served over tomato sauce. You're supposed to eat it with bread but there wasn't any. I had the first bite of the first real salad I had since I got here. It wasn't bad. I would prefer to add some lemon juice and olive oil, but it did the job. The tomatoes had a weird aftertaste.

"Can you taste the tomatoes?" I asked, handing a fork with a piece on it.

She took the fork and tasted it.

"What's wrong?"

"Weird aftertaste?"

"Nah, that's our tomatoes. Get used to it."

"It might be because you grow them underground."

"Maybe."

We ate quietly for a few moments. Was she actually mine? She left Bahomi for me, so could I just be with her without hiding it? Did I even want to be with her? She did manipulate me. But I knew that other than that I could trust her. Or at least I wanted to trust her because I had no one else to trust.

"You know you manipulated me into all this," I said.

It was blunt but I didn't care. The stressful part was over and I could say whatever I wanted, finally.

She looked stunned for a second.

"I had to check if I could trust you."

"By lying to me?" I asked.

"I wasn't lying, I was being friendly."

"You made me think you wanted me so I'd follow you to that room."

"I did."

She smiled. She had something in her teeth. She still looked cute. I pointed to it. She blushed and removed it, lowering her eyes.

"But you were with Bahomi."

She deserved my pushing.

"Not anymore."

She grabbed my hand and made me drop my fork. I was still chewing.

"I can think of something that will help you wake up."

After two minutes we were making up in her room. She literally pressed a button on her bed and there was a door for an inner room that was bigger, with bigger beds.

"What is this?"

"Security measures. The president's family can't be safe in a normal room."

The door closed behind us and we were alone. She kissed my face and neck. I was kind of frozen.

"Anything else that you 'rich and famous' have that I should know of?"

"We can take longer showers."

"Oh, great," I said.

She pushed me into bed and we were making out for real with hands above and beneath the clothes and all. Her tongue was so gentle it made me quiver. She started peeling off my overalls. I had just one more thing that bothered me other than the fact that I was as pale as a corpse.

"What about running away north?"

"What about it?"

She apparently didn't mind me interfering with the questions, and set a gentle hand on my crotch.

"Didn't you say you'd rather live up there than staying here, if you could?"

"I did."

"And?"

It was a bit hard for me to think with her hand stroking me.

"You were right; I didn't know what was up there." She kissed me to hush me. "They have a bigger Purist problem than we do. We saw what happened in Norway."

She started to undress herself. It felt unreal.

"No point of leaving," she finalized.

"Really? That's it?" I asked.

"I'm staying here with you. Is that ok?"

She was now fully naked, sending me an inviting smile. She was mine. Everything I had wanted since I arrived was being given to me.

"What is this? What's happening?" I asked.

"Roy, relax. It's fine."

She leaned over and stroked my cheek.

"This isn't real, the salad, your skin, your tongue, this room." I pushed her away from me. "I can't believe anything you're telling me."

"You're freaking out right know, it's the tranquilizers wearing off."

I jumped in my place.

"The tranquilizers? Your mom assimilated us!"

"She didn't. I talked to her."

"But she did, this isn't real. We're inside right now."

"You're acting crazy."

I looked at her, studying her face.

"Maybe you're not real," I said.

She tried to hug me. I shook her off.

"I need to wake up. I want to wake up!"

I started banging on the wall.

"Roy, relax! This is real!"

I banged on the walls so hard I started to hyperventilate. The light began to change.

"Please listen to me. It's me, and we're finally together. No more secrets."

No matter what she said, it still didn't feel right. The same as my test with Dr. Manu. The simulation didn't get it *just right* and I could feel it. I had been assimilated. I was locked in a dream. She looked at me like I was insane. Her face morphed a little and she looked like Hadar.

"Stay with me," she said softly. Whoever she was.

I had just one more thing to try. I closed my eyes and thought about flying. I imagined myself higher and higher above ground. Inch by inch. I was concentrating and sweating, my overalls hanging from my waist. But I felt resistance, like a gravity but stronger. I kept telling myself it wasn't real and I was about to wake up. I opened my eyes yet I wasn't flying at all. I was still standing on the ground. Nothing had happened.

A second later, I saw a bright white light, and then fell to the ground.

I woke up with a hand holding me down at the shoulder. It was a doctor pointing a syringe at me. Just like the first day. I didn't like the syringe way of communicating, and this time I was stronger and more conscious. The doctor looked shocked when I looked back at him. I grabbed his hand and directed the syringe to the bed frame while I punched him with the other, which knocked him down. I pushed my chest up to release myself from the strap that locked me to the bed, but I failed. So I used all I had and managed to slide under it. It was a good thing I was still skinny. I took out the IV needle in my arm and the urine collector from my pants. Then I stood up, dizzy, and held the bed frame until I got my senses together. He was about to rise again so I kicked his stomach, causing him to wiggle around like a worm. I saw the room's door was open, and I looked to the other side. Shanta, Bahomi, and the rest were all assimilated.

An alarm sounded. Red lights flickered. I had to wake them up before someone else came. The doctor on the floor began to move so I stuck the syringe in his neck and he collapsed. I opened Shanta's bed and woke her up, and then I did the

same for Toya and Dev. I stopped before I opened
Bahomi's bed. Should I raise that asshole? He
thought I was responsible. But we needed everyone
and he was the best fighter. I opened his bed and
woke him up gentler so it'd take longer. Then I
went to the last bed. It was Dr. Manu, who had
tested my skills. He was our inside man? The chief
engineer was the guy? I woke him up and went back
to the others and shook them a little more. The red
light and the siren did the rest. Then I went to see
Shanta. I could have had her just a moment ago, yet
it wasn't real. She was real now but she wasn't mine
anymore.

"We were assimilated, we have to run!" I
shouted to them while they woke up.

Shanta looked at me frightened, like I turned
her most delicate dream directly into a nightmare.
Which was probably true.

"No time now, we have to go."

We all ran to the secret room as fast as we
could without the guards spotting us. We reached
the room, gasping for air. After a few seconds
Shanta started to talk.

"How did you wake up? No one wakes up from this."

Then I felt a sharp pain on the back of my skull and I collapsed.

"I'll kill you. I'll fucking kill you," I heard Bahomi shout.

Bahomi stood above me, kicking my ribs. I heard one of them crack. Dev came to my aid and was strong in comparison to someone just waking up from assimilated sleep.

"Don't you see what he has done?" Bahomi shouted while Dev held him against the wall.

"It's not his fault, he got caught, too," Shanta said in my defense.

"He brought her to us!"

Shanta and the rest looked at me.

"I didn't."

I was in so much pain that I couldn't speak much.

"He just freed you from assimilation, you idiot!" Shanta shouted.

"We don't…have time," I said in pain.

Toya helped me up. It was a weird picture. Dev was retraining an enraged Bahomi while Toya was holding me up, with Shanta standing in the middle.

"Let me go!" Bahomi shook Dev off and stood next to the door facing us.

"I'm sick of your stupid plans over plans and never-ending contemplation," Bahomi erupted with anger. "If it wasn't for him, we'd be still on our original course!"

He swung his right arm at my face, but I pulled back.

"If it wasn't for you, we'd actually have a course!" he yelled.

He swung his fist again and I ducked under it, trying to make him angrier so he'd lose focus.

"You rat! You sold us out!"

This time he caught me with a kick to the ribs. I held onto his leg and punched his throat. He caved in and started coughing. Then I tried to grab him by the neck and push him to the floor, but he released himself with an elbow to my ribs. I heard another rib crack, or maybe it was the same one.

He stood up, still coughing. He looked at Shanta and said. "Is this what you want, this pacifist peace of shit? You know he let the Purist go? He just let him go."

"How do you know that?" I asked. "You were out on the ground."

"I should have left you there," Bahomi said.

I lunged at him, shooting my fists at his face, trying to hold his neck. He got me in the ribs over and over again. The pain was almost stunning, but my rage and adrenaline soothed it from paralyzing my body. I grabbed his neck and started to strangle him.

"I should have let him bash your head on the ground," I said through clenched teeth.

In that moment, that's exactly what I did. I pulled Bahomi's neck and pushed it back into the wall behind him. Before I knew it, his face was turning blue.

"Stop! You're killing him!" Shanta yelled.

She stopped me at the last moment, pulling at my arms.

She unclenched my hands, freeing Bahomi. He was almost unable to breathe. I was furious and I tried to get back in position but Shanta was in my way.

"Both of you stop!" she said.

"Enjoy your last minutes of peace," Bahomi laboredly whispered.

Then he ran away.

"Where does he think he can go?" I asked. "They will catch him and find us."

"I don't know," Shanta replied.

My rib was pulsing with pain. It hurt every time I took a breath.

"Find him before he does something stupid," Shanta commanded Dev, who then rushed out of the room. "Make sure no one sees you!"

Dr. Manu looked at me and smiled.

"Glad you didn't take the janitor job."

He knew. That son of a bitch knew. He drilled me hard to tip me to the resistance's side.

"We can't all go out like nothing happened," he said.

"We can't stay here either," Shanta said.

Was Manu the one pulling her strings?

"We can go to the gunroom," I advised.

"And then what? We're trapped again with no water or food," said Toya.

"Food and water are no problem," said Dr. Manu, "I can reroute the pipes."

"They will search for us there," added Shanta.

The alarm was still blaring. They could've come at any moment. We were all looking at each other, clueless. What could we do next? Bahomi was on the loose with crazy eyes, and we were exposed. All our plans had turned to garbage, and we knew it.

Then the power dropped entirely. No light, no air conditioning, not even the emergency lighting kicked on. Complete silence and blackness.

"That's odd," said Dr. Manu. "It doesn't look like the backup generators are working."

Chapter 16

The power was still down and the air was getting heavy and sticky.

"If the backup generators don't start in a minute, it's going to get really hot in here," said Dr. Manu.

"Purists, I'm assuming. Great timing," I said.

Suddenly Shanta snapped.

"It's Bahomi. He's waking everyone up and disconnecting the simulators' backup generators. This is the old plan."

"If he disconnected the wrong ones it means there aren't backup generators for security either," said Dr. Manu. "I have to go."

Who knew how many of these people had actually left the simulation to walk around Knaan in the past week, month or even year? Now they'd wake up in complete darkness and almost definitely panic. The silence and confusion would turn into frustration, which would quickly turn into panic and angry screams and demands for answers.

We started hearing the commotion through the pipes and air tunnels. The bursts of sounds became more frequent, yet after a few moments the AC started working again. So did the emergency lights. The PA system rattled.

"This is President Padma. We're fixing this problem. Please remain calm and stay in your rooms."

I was sure Padma's attempt to sooth the panic wouldn't work. Predictably, we started hearing muffled explosions from above, like a fireworks show in a nearby city. I looked at Shanta.

"The invasion," I said, "they waited for the moment our systems break."

"We're not ready," she said.

"We need guns."

"I can get you guns."

"I need you with me. We need to talk to your mom right now."

I looked at Toya.

"Get us as many guns and as many magazines as you can carry, and meet us at the security room."

They took off. Shanta and I sprinted to the security room. I could tell she had difficulty grasping the concept of her plan going south thanks to Bahomi. We ran up the stairs amidst the sounds of explosions and panicked shouting.

"People of Knaan. Please remain calm. Our security system is handling the situation."

Thank you, Bahomi, for rushing the apocalypse.

We came next to the security room. There were many other people there, all dressed in white overalls. They were pale and skinny, and some were hairless. They were looking for answers. The door was shut and two guards with guns stood by it. We pushed through the crowd until we reached the door.

"Mom!" Shanta shouted.

"You need us!"

The guards looked baffled. They probably didn't know about the resistance. That was something Padma would never share in a PA announcement.

"Let us in!"

She demanded one of the guards open the door, and, although he recognized her, he didn't know what to do.

"I'm sorry. President's orders."

The other talked into his comms device, and the door soon opened and Padma emerged. She looked at us, raging.

"*Catch them!*" she commanded.

We couldn't escape because the crowd was pushing against us, and the guards held us with their guns against our chests.

"*You need us. We're the only ones that know how to fight,*" Shanta said.

Then a voice from the inside reported: "*All sentinels down. Ten cameras down.*"

I said to Padma, "You can't let them near the openings."

"*Take them back to assimilation and make sure they're locked this time.*"

Toya and Dev rushed in with guns, and pointed them at Padma.

"*Release them!*" Dev said.

Looking furious, Padma briefly paused, but then ordered them to let us go.

Toya and Dev handed us guns.

"*What do you want?*" Padma asked.

"*President Padma, we need you here,*" a voice from inside the security room demanded.

"You must fire at a higher rate to keep them away from the hatch openings!" I shouted.

Padma reluctantly listened. She looked like she knew she was running out of options.

"We're already doing that…what else?"

"Give people guns," I said.

"Out of the question."

The muffled explosions sounded louder and nearer.

"You want it to be like twenty years ago? The people MUST defend themselves."

"President Padma, we need you here, now!"

A loud alarm sounded.

"This is a security announcement: please remain in your beds and close the doors."

The people of the crowd ran amok. Padma's face was white. She went inside and closed the door. I looked at Shanta for a clue.

"We've been breached."

Before I managed to say anything else, shots rang out from below, so we ran downstairs. In the main street people were screaming and trying to run for cover, pushing each other and falling over. But the shots didn't stop. We followed the noise and I finally saw two men with guns shooting at people. They were dressed in something that looked like a Cactus suit but lighter, like it was made out of shiny silk. They looked like they had gas masks on, at least from what I could tell, since they were facing the opposite direction. I aimed my gun at them and shot two bullets, one in each of their heads. They collapsed. The dead bodies of the city's guards were strewn out in front of them, and there was blood everywhere. The room went silent for a second as people didn't understand who was firing at whom.

Then the chaos rose again.

"*Doctors! Where are the doctors?!*" someone shouted.

I took a quick look, and there were about twenty dead bodies on the ground, and even more wounded. Then the smoke started rolling in. It burned. It was tear gas being piped in from the AC system.

"Shanta, they're trying to scare us out."

I coughed, and my eyes and nose ran. My vision blurred.

"Tell them to ask for whoever shot a gun in the simulation to report to the ammo room. Go!"

Shanta, Dev and Toya ran back to where we came from. I hoped she could convince her mom to listen.

The AC fans stopped and then started to work in reverse direction, sucking the tear gas out. I heard more gunshots from two different directions, then explosions.

I started running in the direction of the explosions, and then realized the zip lines on the ceiling could get me there faster. I grabbed a handle. A line on the floor became red and I swung through the main street and raised my gun. Four Purists came into my field of view. They were breaking down doors and shooting everyone inside the rooms. I shot them while swinging by. Blood splattered everywhere. I swung all the way around, taking the Purists by surprise and shooting them in the back. The magazine ran empty.

People started carrying the wounded to the clinic. More tear gas poured in. The AC wasn't strong enough to suck everything out. I needed more ammo, so I went through the inner circle to the ammo room. Shanta, Dev and Toya were there handing guns to a crowd of kids. I looked at Shanta and she flashed a grin, seeing that I was alive.

"How many guns do we have?" I asked Shanta.

"About a hundred."

"That's all? What about magazines?"

She pointed at four crates of loaded magazines and more crates of bullets and empty magazines. It wasn't enough. I took five teens with me and showed them in which direction to load the bullets into the magazine.

"Don't stop until you can't push it down any more. Load these as fast as you can."

"All of you, listen! We might not have another chance to reload, so listen carefully!"

All the teens looked at me with puppy eyes, young and innocent. Yet full of adrenaline and hormones, ready to prove themselves.

"Save your bullets. Only one shot to the chest. When you aim, stay still and exhale."

It didn't seem real at all but that's all we had: teenagers defending the underground city.

Purists were coming in by the dozens.

"I have an idea," I said to Shanta, grabbing her by the hand. The teens would buy us the time.

"Where are we going?!" she shouted.

"To the clinic, I need Viti's help."

We ran like crazy. The sound of gunfire was constant by now. When we reached the door to the main street we kneeled and looked at each other.

"You can do it," I said as we pushed the door and aimed at both directions.

Bullets whizzed past so we immediately closed the door.

"Shit shit shit."

"Let's find another way," she said.

I nodded.

She turned around but I kept my eyes on the door. She helped guide me as I walked backwards. Then the door cracked open and a grenade rolled in.

"GRENADE!" I shouted.

We ran past a corner and ducked behind it. The grenade exploded and the echo from the corridor made our ears ring. I lunged out from behind the corner, but there was no one there. Then the door opened and I shot a Purist right in the heart. Another one came through, whom I shot in the head.

"Come!" I told Shanta but she didn't listen. She was petrified.

I pulled her over and we went back again to the main street, stepping on the Purists' bodies. We took their gas masks and continued to the clinic. The clinic was guarded heavily by ten teenagers and two guards. They had turned the cryo cylinders into shields. I hoped those were thick enough.

They let us inside the clinic. It was chaotic. I only saw about eight doctors and there were more than fifty people stacked inside. Wounded people lay on the floor waiting for care. I went to Viti's room. She was by now eight months pregnant. She was standing there trying to calm down another pregnant woman who'd been shot in the leg.

"Viti!"

"Roy! Are you hurt?"

"No I'm fine. I need your help."

"Sure." Her eyes lit up.

"Can you plug a laser gun inside the main street?"

"Technically yes…depends on the voltage."

"Will it connect to the emergency zip line?"

She took a moment to calculate it all in her head.

"I can do it, but it won't shoot as strong as it normally shoots."

"Laser shot to the head from 10 feet away isn't strong enough?"

She smiled. "That would do."

We walked as fast as we could with a pregnant woman on-board. Two more kids escorted us through the inner corridors of the city. The kids were close to Viti, helping her walk. I was at the front and Shanta held up the rear. We reached the gunroom and locked the door behind us. Viti immediately got to work. There was a functional gun on the table. Viti tore the lid from the gun and started pulling some wires and electric boards. She worked so fast. She cut away some plugs. Then she was left with two exposed wires and a loose electric circuit in her hand.

"Let's go," she said.

"I don't remember where I left the zip line," I said.

"Don't worry."

I was again in the front and Shanta again in the rear. One boy carried the laser gun and the other helped Viti. We reached the main street. It smelled like drying blood and burned flesh. Shots were fired every few seconds. Screams of pain pierced our ears. Shanta approached the wall and pressed on a button, and the handle for the zip line came flying in.

"Open the box," Viti said, grabbing the handle.

I took the end of a gun and busted opened the handle's electric box.

"See the red and black wires? Expose them right in the middle. Don't touch anything else."

I was taller than she was, so I had to do it myself. She handed me the cutter and I trusted her I that wouldn't get electrocuted.

"Good, now attach it with this one," she said, handing me the laser gun's exposed wire. I crossed all three wire ends together.

Shots were fired at us and we all ducked to the floor. Viti Landed on her belly and screeched in pain. I shot back but there was no one standing there. The boy who held the laser gun had been shot in the chest. His blood was all over the floor. And then they came back, so Shanta, the other kid and I fired back. We took down five of them. I looked at Viti. She was terrified. She stood up and her belly was all red.

"Is it my blood?" she asked, panicked.

"I don't know," I answered and I looked at the floor in order to trace the blood from the boy's chest to her stomach. But it was indeed hers. They had shot her right in the belly.

She burst into tears. She became hysterical.

"Take her to the clinic!" I ordered Shanta and the kid.

Shanta grabbed her by the hand, and so did the boy.

"No!" Viti cried in terror.

"I can do it. Go!"

Shanta and the kid took Viti to the clinic.

I was alone.

My eyes were wet, and my hands were bloody. I lost grip of the laser gun twice before I held it high enough to reach the other wire. The black wire was slippery and I couldn't expose it because I had no grip. Bullets whizzed all around me. There was a Purist taking cover behind the street's curve. I dropped to the floor again and fired back. I ran out of ammo so I took the gun off the dead kid. Shots bounced off the laser gun cover. I hoped it wasn't damaged. I shot back and killed another Purist. I wiped my hands on my clothes and stood up again, balancing the laser gun between my shoulder and my cheek. I was finally able to close the circuit. The lights on the gun blinked. I could see it was only loading to a fourth of the energy capacity, but that would have to do. I held the gun under my right armpit and the electric board underneath it in my hand. I grabbed the handle and I swung forward through the main street. I aimed for the guys in silk, and they didn't even see me coming. And when they did it was too late, because I'd already scorched a hole in their chests. The gun loaded quickly because it only used a fourth of its capacity, yet since I fired it so close to my targets it caused severe damage.

I killed almost ten Purists when I lost grip. I fell onto the floor and the laser gun banged on my head. I immediately got my shit together and switched hands. My head was bleeding. I held the

Laser gun under my left armpit and grabbed the handles with the right. I was exhausted and shaking and blood dripped into my eyes. I completed another semicircle and killed about twenty more Purists. By now, the street was filled with bodies of both Purists and Knaan citizens.

Things started quieting down. At one point I didn't hear a gunshot for over a minute. I disconnected the laser gun and hid it behind a simulation bed of the nearest room. I took a gun that was on the floor, and checked to see if it had bullets left. It did. I went into the clinic. There were only four guarding it now. Shanta was one of them.

"Viti?" I asked.

"The baby," she said, and I could see the tears in her eyes.

"We killed her baby!" she screamed and I held her tight. I didn't know what to do.

She looked at me and saw my head wound.

"Inside..." she said, sobbing.

We went inside. It was more chaotic than when I'd left. We could barely move. I hoped more people had come to the clinic looking for a place to hide, instead of being wounded. Dr. Ashish came to look at me.

"Press here," he said to Shanta. She pressed my wound with a bandage. And he went to get something.

"Did you see Bahomi at all?" I asked her.

"One of the teens said there was one group fighting outside."

"Toya and Dev?"

Ashish came back and stitched my head.

"I don't know." She burst into tears again.

My eyes started to wet and I wiped them. Ashish finished and left to tend to other people.

"We need to find Bahomi. This isn't over yet."

"Yeah," she said.

Suddenly the lights went out. Everyone screamed in panic.

"This is President Padma speaking." She sounded choked up over the PA system. *"The Nature Purification Organization has captured me and the security team."*

The screams intensified.

"They control the city. We are now their hostages. Their leader promised me that no harm will be done to us if we all cooperate and do as they say. Please evacuate the city in an orderly fashion."

"We need to get to her," Shanta said.

She grabbed my arm but I was exhausted. Bloody. It was over. They won. We weren't prepared. It wasn't enough.

"We need to help her!" she screamed. "Get up, soldier!"

"It's pointless...we're outnumbered...we failed..."

"Help me save her!"

She grabbed me and put a gun in my hand. I staggered to my feet and followed her out. Then the PA system was turned on again.

"I'm sorry I failed you, my children."

Then we heard a gunshot.

"NO!" Shanta screamed in tears.

The AC stopped. Tear gas flowed in again. We both put on our gas masks. People started running outside. The eye windows were all foggy and I couldn't see Shanta.

"Stop, don't go there!" I shouted at the people. "It's a trap!" I shouted but no one could hear me through the masks. It was pointless to try and save everyone. I held Shanta while she cried. Then a large, metal grinding sound filled the main street and a strange light filled the space around us.

"They're opening the main door," I said to Shanta with a shattered voice.

"They're...leading them...out."

Then I broke into tears, my mask became foggy and I couldn't see anything. They'd killed Viti's kid, Padma was dead and the Purists were winning. There was nothing else to do. We failed. I failed. I didn't train them well enough, I wasn't a leader. I shouldn't have come back to shower, I shouldn't have told Isaac anything, I shouldn't have fallen in love with Shanta. I shouldn't have gone out with Bahomi, I shouldn't have wanted to fit in. If I'd become a storyteller none of this would have happened. I killed Viti's kid by asking her to help us, and now all the people are running out to their death.

I was breathing heavy inside the mask and holding Shanta. She was shivering. And then Isaac's mantra arose in my mind: *"I shall grow old and die, all the people I love will fade away, everything is changing, and everything is connected."* And then I just let go. There was nothing for me to achieve anymore, I will die one day anyway. I'd lost the people I loved anyway—so I failed them, too—everything was already changing in front of me, and everything was connected and I just couldn't control it all by myself.

When everything was gone and I had reached rock-bottom, there was nothing else left but Knaan's people. I could still try to save them. Nothing else mattered anymore, not my life, not my parents, not Padma's, not Viti's, not Shanta's, Toya's, Dev's or Bahomi's. I could still try to save the people. And if I die trying, it wouldn't matter because I already died once and I will die again. I felt my body getting energetic again, my strength returning. Shanta noticed it and sat next to me.

"Follow me," I said and grabbed Shanta by the hand. She felt so tired and heavy. We had to walk through the current of people. They were trying to escape the gas, not knowing they were being led to their deaths.

We walked to the water corridor where Bahomi had led me before. The air was cool. The gas hadn't gotten there so we took off our gas masks, gasping for fresh air. We were thirsty and tired and hurting.

"What are we going to do?" She asked me.

"I have an idea but we have to go outside."

We kept walking for another minute until we reached the hatch. Bahomi was lying there next to a pile of dead Purists. He was badly hurt. Gunshot to the stomach. He sat in a pool of blood holding his gun.

"*I guarded the hatch,*" he said, smiling, "*I killed so many of them.*"

Shanta looked at him with disgust.

"*Take me to the clinic, please.*"

Her face contorted, and she raised her gun. I wasn't fast enough to stop what was about to happen.

"This is your fault," Shanta said, and shot him in the head. His brains splattered onto the wall and all over Shanta's face and clothes.

"And this is for my mom."

She then spat on his corpse and started crying. I controlled a gag reflex. She was scary and powerful and I had nothing to say. But this wasn't over yet. We put on the Cactus suits that were stashed there and went out of the hatch to plan ahead.

Chapter 17

The sun was setting and more people poured out of the city's smoking mouth. There stood thousands of people in white overalls, pale and skinny. The useless army of the numb, without a home and without a leader.

We snuck around in our Cactus suits.

"My brothers are still there, and so are my friends," said Shanta.

"So are Isaac and his wife, and Viti and her husband. I hope they are alive."

"What's your plan?" she asked.

"The Purists can just kill them all right there, but they haven't."

One of the Purists stood up on a boulder. He looked like a healthy, built version of Knaan people. Like he escaped and got a tan and grew stubble. It took me a second to realize he was the same Purist leader from the video twenty years ago. Purist soldiers surrounded the crowd and aimed directly at the people. Each Purist was wearing the same thin Cactus suit. Other Purist soldiers pulled random people from the first line and took them up the hill in front of the crowd.

"Your city is ours!" he shouted. His voice was carried away to a distance with no trees to stop it. "Your **technology** is useless, **you** are useless, and your president is **dead**."

There was a loud commotion in the crowd. He raised his hand and one of the soldiers shot an old man who'd been carried away to the hill. The crowd went completely quiet.

"Do not say a word. Disobey me and we'll shoot another one of yours. If you wish to survive do exactly as I say." He paused and looked at the crowd. He must have felt like a god.

"If you're an energy, water or food technician, raise your hand."

No one lifted a finger. He raised his hand again and a woman was shot. Her body rolled down the hill. Next in line was a teenage boy.

"If you are a water, energy or food technician, raise your hand."

Hands lifted.

"Go stand next to the main gate."

People started to move. There were whispers and quiet crying.

"SILENCE!"

He raised his hand again and the teenage boy fell to his death along with two other men who were kneeling next to him.

"They need the people who'll maintain the systems for them," Shanta said.

"So what if there were no functional systems left?" I said.

"If we destroy the systems no one will survive."

"So then we need to kill the Purists first."

"How many are they?"

"A lot."

I paused to think because something in the picture before my eyes was wrong.

"If we can split them up somehow," I said, "maybe the rest could help us. We are outgunned but not outnumbered." There were thousands of scared people being held by maybe a couple hundred gunmen.

"Look at them, how can THEY help us?"

"It's our only chance. Let's release the food," I said with a grin.

We snuck back inside, walking as fast as we could without making a sound. We jumped over bodies so we didn't slide on the blood. All lights were off except the emergency lights. With no AC the smell and heat were horrible. Flies now circled the bodies.

We finally got down to the room full of bug containers. The control panel showed near-maximum capacity.

"So, what do we expect should happen?" Shanta asked.

"The cockroaches need to follow the light and swamp the crowd."

"And then we charge the Purists and hope the people will follow."

"Simple."

She turned to me and held my hand. Her hand was dirty with dry blood.

"I'm sorry I got you into this, I had no other option."

"Ahh, I do this all the time," I smiled.

"I'm also **not** sorry because without you everything would be shitball soup."

"It's a shitball soup anyway."

"We might die."

"We might."

"Anyway, it was nice knowing you."

"You, too."

We faced each other for a beat and then looked at the container.

"How do we break this open?" she asked.

I saw a pipe wrench lying on a tool rack and brought it to the container. I opened a sliding door and saw the disgusting festival inside though a square glass window. It looked like the right place to plant my wrench.

"Let's hope they follow the light."

"Ok, on the count of three, and then we run to the hatch."

"Sounds like a suicide plan."

"Do we have enough ammo?

"Probably not."

"Ok," I said, and took a deep breath. I lifted the wrench: "One...two...three..."

I swung the wrench into the glass and it shattered inwards. It took less than a millisecond for the roaches to realize there was an opening. They poured out like a river of sewage overflowing the street. We ran like crazy. The bugs clung to our clothes, crawling inside our sleeves. It was the worst sensation I have ever experienced. I wanted to puke out of every pore in my skin. We ran and shook our bodies until we reached the hatch. We put on the Cactus suits and climbed up as fast as we could and closed the hatch. We were still scratching our bodies and picking out bugs. The hatch was far enough from the people. No one had noticed us. We started crawling on our stomachs toward the crowd. In a normal day we would get shot in a millisecond, but the security system was down and the cameras were broken. Our Cactus suits quickly filled with the sand we were crawling on. We hid behind a rock and watched as the Purist leader raised his hand and shot another group of people. He was sorting out the ones he needed, making the others more and more submissive. By Bahomi's stories, he might order them to kill each other to sort out the fittest to convert.

"Come on. Where are they?" I whispered.

"Any second now."

And then we saw it, like a stain of oil spreading on a yellow ocean. Millions of bugs poured out of the main gate in any direction possible. The Purists were surprised. People started to shout.

"STOP THE LEAK!" the Purist leader yelled. He ordered five soldiers to go inside. They hesitated, so he shot one of them. The rest ran inside. The crowd started to back away from the main gate.

"STOP!" the leader yelled, shooting at the crowd. People fell down.

As the bugs came closer and closer, the Purist soldiers began to look nervous.

"They're not splitting up," Shanta said.

"It's too late."

I was afraid, and my body was filled with adrenaline. I'd lost it all anyway, and had nothing else to lose.

We waited just a few more seconds until the four Purists vanished inside the city's mouth. And then we stood up and cocked our guns and started to run into the crowd. The Purist didn't see us until we started to fire. We took out three of them. We continued running.

"STOMP THEM! WE ARE THOUSANDS! PICK UP A ROCK AND KILL THE PURISTS FOR YOUR FAMILIES! FOR PRESIDENT PADMA!" I yelled.

We shot more at the Purists before the crowd devoured them. The first rows of people got hit by the Purists' shots but in a few seconds the guns were torn off their hands. The Purists were pushed to the ground and stomped by the thousands of furious legs of the united numb army. They bashed their heads with rocks. They shot them with their own guns. They cracked their bones and tore their flesh. The people of Knaan felt the power of the mass for the first time ever. I saw the Purist leader running away and I shot at him, but I missed. I tore the Cactus suit off and started to run after him up the hill, to the same place Bahomi took me to watch over the Purist city. I shot three more times, all missed during my run. As soon as he was across the hill I realized this time I wasn't going to have mercy. With my last strength I ran up the hill and

planted myself on the ground like a sniper. I shot
him while he was running down towards the Purist
camp, yet missed again. I threw the gun to the
ground and tossed my body off the ridge. I started
spinning and spinning like a barrel down the hill.
My head hit the rocks and my back felt like it was
about to break. I rolled and rolled until I crashed
into him at the foot of the hill. He screamed in pain.
I put my thumbs in his eyes and clung to his head
while thrusting it into the ground. He screamed like
a wounded animal. He screamed until his skull
cracked and he stopped moving. I pulled my fingers
from his bloody eye sockets and didn't look back.

When I came down the hill on Knaan's side I
saw the Purists were flattened on the ground and
were covered in dirt. People screamed from
excitement. People cried from sadness and joy.
Many of us had died but thousands would live on.

The last rays of sun painted the sky with
yellow, green and blue. Darkness was taking over.
The bugs had dispersed. We had no food and no
security. Shanta climbed onto the boulder on which
the Purist leader stood just a moment ago.

"I am Shanta, daughter of President Padma. We have a lot to do. Care for our wounded. Bury our dead. Clean our city and restore its systems. Whoever has a technical job, please take care of your post. The others should take care of their rooms and surrounding corridors."

She looked at me and extended her hand. I reached out and got on the boulder.

"This is Roy. The GTA. Without him, we'd all be dead."

They cheered for us from the top of their lungs, and people hugged and cried and screamed with joy.

I smiled at her, and she smiled back. We stepped down from the boulder and went back inside. Every senior technician gathered their staff and went inside to fix the systems. People worked all night to restore the city to normality. Shanta eventually found her brothers.

We were safe at last.

Chapter 18 – EPILOGUE

I thought I'd have nightmares but I slept like a baby that night. Maybe I was just suppressing everything because my body was so tired and weak from fighting. A lot of people had gotten dehydrated during the stay outside. They portioned the algae so everyone could eat something, and started collecting bugs to reinsert into the container. Also, I'd found out that there was a smaller reserve container just for situations like this.

It was a new day of freedom but for the first time I didn't know what to do. There was no training. No plans to plot. So I just went to the gunroom and helped the former gun technicians fix the broken guns as fast as possible. Some had taken direct hits and exploded into pieces. Isaac came by and introduced me to his wife. After everything that happened he decided that she was going to stay with him outside the simulation. Shanta's brothers were not harmed, and she was their sole caretaker at this point. Toya and Dev were dead. Knaan made the chief security officer president, and Dr. Manu was in charge of the whole restoration process. No one knew about the resistance. Only three of us remained to tell about how we wanted to save the city, yet had to destroy it first. I guess that summed it up. Bahomi got his glory after all by guarding the hatch and dying for the cause. Yet, in the city he'd always remain the one who destroyed it. Isaac had a new story to tell the children, a story with the moral of always being prepared and not counting on the systems.

While walking in the city I could hear people talking about going to the northern city. They thought Knaan wasn't safe anymore and that they'd never be able to fix everything fast enough. And that the remaining Purists would retaliate. I could stay and help rebuild the city; everyone respected me because I'd earned my place. On the other hand, if I reached the northern city I might be able to find out more about my parents. This would be the best time to leave because the Purists suffered a massive blow and would take long to recover. I told Shanta about my idea, but she came up with a third option. During the attack our security team sent a distress call for the northern city, but Monish from the floating city picked up on it and they were on their way to help.

"Why would they want to help us?" I asked.

"They are willing to take us north to Scandinavia where you can still walk outside without melting."

"Are you sure it's safe there? What about Purists over there? What about their resources? Who says we can trust these rich folks?"

"The way I see it, you have two options," Shanta said, "because staying here is suicide. The last thing I'll do is stay in this place or one like it. If yesterday didn't make that point clear."

She got close to me and held both of my hands.

"If you stay here you will continue to fix guns for the rest of your life. Then one day you'll retire and choose to assimilate because that's what everybody does eventually. Or you can go on a dangerous road to the northern city. Your job will be to protect a large group of people who never lived above ground. Once you reach there, you'll have to start over just like you did here. Plus the chance of finding your parents is below zero."

"I know that," I said after taking a deep sigh.

"But you have another option. You can come with me and the people you trust to a place that actually has a future to offer you. What will it be?"

"Leave it all behind after we almost died to protect it?"

"It was never my intention to stay. Ask yourself if you would have."

"How do you know this floating city isn't just another techno-prison you'll live to hate? How different is it from this place?"

"I don't know. But I know that the northern city is just the same as Knaan and I'm staying in neither."

"At least we know what we're dealing with, though."

"Your parents are dead! Face it. I'm sorry, but you're going to kill yourself and you won't find them. We just stopped a Purist attack, but there will be more. Nothing has actually changed. But we can change *our* future if we go away to a place where there's hope. My mom trusted these people and so do I."

"Just say you want me to come with you."

"I want you to come with me."

We hugged deeply, breathing into each other.
Like our hearts melted and welded together. We
were alone in the world, but we had each other now.

I chose to come with her to the floating city. I
chose the unknown hope over known false stability.

Oh, I was so wrong.

Thank you for reading my debut novel!

I hope it stirred something in you.

If you like this book please let me know by leaving a review on Amazon or Goodreads.

P.S. You can also subscribe to my mailing list at moranchaim.com for updates and special gifts about the upcoming books of the Cryonemesis series.

P.S.S. you can ask me anything on: moranchaimbooks@gmail.com